Andrews McMeel Publishing
a division of Andrews McMeel Universal
1130 Walnut Street, Kansas City, Missouri 64106

www.andrewsmcmeel.com

23 24 25 26 27 KRP 10 9 8 7 6 5 4 3 2 1

ISBN: 978-1-5248-8960-9
Library of Congress Control Number: 2023943970

Editor: Erinn Pascal
Designer: Jessica Rodriguez
Production Editor: Margaret Utz and David Shaw
Production Manager: Chadd Keim

ATTENTION: SCHOOLS AND BUSINESSES

Andrews McMeel books are available at quantity discounts with
bulk purchase for educational, business, or sales promotional use.
For information, please e-mail the Andrews McMeel Publishing
Special Sales Department: sales@amuniversal.com

DREAMWORKS

KUNG FU PANDA 4

THE MOVIE NOVEL

ADAPTED BY
JUNE DAY

Andrews McMeel
PUBLISHING®

CONTENTS

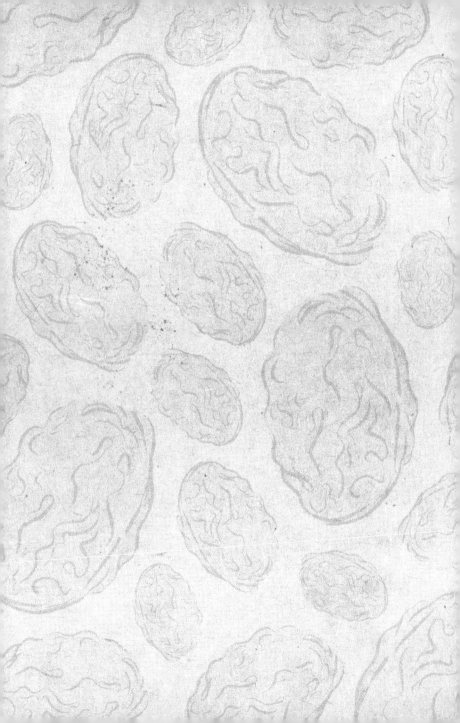

"Every pit
holds the strength
of a mighty tree."

PROLOGUE

High up in the frigid snow-capped mountains, in an otherwise desolate terrain, was an iron quarry. It was lit by a few lanterns, nothing more.

A few rams mined the quarry, hoping to extract as much iron as possible. They carried poles and lugged wheelbarrows filled with iron weapons and tools.

One ram, who looked particularly frightened, pushed his wheelbarrow toward the opening of the pit. He bleated a greeting to his supervisor, who was also a ram. The supervisor bleated back. Rams, as it turns out, like to bleat hello.

The ram peered into the quarry. It was a tunnel with no end in sight. Then—***ZZRP!***—his lamp and all the other lanterns fizzled out. Darkness filled the space.

Then, there was a low growl, a rumbling from within the quarry. The ram squinted and saw it was coming from a large, shadowy figure with bright yellow eyes. Suddenly . . .

ROAR!!!

A cry—powerful and dangerous—echoed out of the pit as the ram miner backed away in horror.

The figure appeared out of the darkness.

"That's right," the figure said very menacingly. "It is I . . . Tai Lung!"

Tai Lung was a fierce warrior who was trained in kung fu by the great Master Shifu. After he was denied the role of Dragon Warrior, he revealed his dark nature by attacking the Valley of Peace.

"It can't be!" the supervisor said. "The Dragon Warrior banished Tai Lung to the Spirit Realm."

This had happened many years ago. The Dragon Warrior, Po, had performed an advanced and powerful kung fu move called the Wuxi Finger Hold on the evil snow leopard Tai Lung. With a flex of his pinky finger and the word "*Skadoosh*," the Dragon Warrior had defeated Tai Lung for good . . . or so everyone had thought.

But here Tai Lung stood powerful as ever.

"I have returned to take what is mine . . . which is everything that is *yours*," Tai Lung said menacingly. He lunged for a wheelbarrow and threw it into a large spinning wheel. The wheel crashed down and sped through the quarry, creating a trail of fire along its way.

The ram miners screamed as the fire spread.

Tai Lung observed the destruction.

"Let it be known from the highest mountain to the lowest valley," Tai Lung decreed, "that Tai Lung lives, and no one will stand in his way—not even the great Dragon Warrior!"

CHAPTER 1

In the Valley of Peace, the noodle restaurant was bustling with energy. Mr. Ping, dressed in a panda costume, paced nervously back and forth as the size of the crowd continued to increase.

"Po! Where is Po? He was supposed to be here hours ago!" Mr. Ping huffed.

"Ping, will you please just relax? He's on panda time," came a voice. It was Li, who was also a panda. Mr. Ping and Li were Po's dads.

Mr. Ping scoffed at the phrase "panda time." He believed it was just a term that Li and Po had made up in order to sleep until noon.

"But what if he's sick?" Mr. Ping worried. "What if he's hurt? What if he's *hungry*? My baby!"

"Don't get your noodles in a twist. If I know our son, he's probably just kicking back and catching some rays," Li assured him.

Po sure was *catching some rays* all right.

Po soared through the air in an awesome kung fu move. He approached his opponent, a giant stingray, and continued to unleash a series of epic kung fu moves. The stingray spun in midair and smashed right through the dock where they were fighting.

The stingray launched himself back on an attack from the water, but Po jumped from dock pillar to dock pillar, expertly landing on the next one as the stingray destroyed the one prior. Po maneuvered himself into a handstand to stay clear of the water. Unlike stingrays, pandas don't excel underwater.

The stingray wouldn't give up. It tried another move, this time reducing the dock to a single pillar in the water. Po used both hands to balance on the pillar, seemingly cornered.

"Ahhh!" Po screamed.

The stingray circled around Po ominously, like a predator closing in on its prey.

A group of pigs, safe on the shore, watched from behind a stack of crates. Then the stingray launched itself out of the water and spun in midair.

"Oink!" The pigs were not so safe on the shore after all. They fled for cover further from the dock.

But Po wasn't scared. He steadied himself and sprung off the pillar. He soared past the stingray and caught hold of its tail.

"Okay, big guy, we're really gonna have to wrap this up," Po said. He tied the stingray up into a neat bow. "Next time, keep your surf off my turf!"

The pigs emerged from their hiding spots and burst into loud cheers.

"Yeah! Woooo!" the pigs squealed.

Po chuckled. He'd defended the pigs' kelp farm against the stingray. He was the Dragon Warrior, after all—a legendary master of kung fu with limitless power. Saving kelp farms from evil stingrays was exactly why there was a celebration honoring him at his dads' noodle restaurant—

The celebration at his dads' noodle restaurant!

"Uh-oh," Po gulped.

He was late!

CHAPTER 2

Po raced into town. As he made his way to the noodle restaurant, a thicket of adoring fans called out to him.

"It's the Dragon Warrior!" yelled someone in the crowd.

"We love you, Dragon Warrior!" said another.

"Oh, and I love you, too, adoring fan!" Po called out.

Cheers, smiles, and waves followed Po's every step. Po couldn't help himself; he loved the attention. He high-fived a few of his fans.

"Sign my scroll!"

"Sign my shirt!"

"Sign my hat!"

"Okay, okay," replied Po. "I'll sign whatever you want."

Fans closed in to get in on the excitement. Po wasn't even paying attention to what he was signing when suddenly . . .

"Po!"

Po's teacher, Master Shifu, stood before him, looking unamused. Scrawled across Master Shifu's unamused face was Po's autograph.

Po attempted to wipe the autograph off his trainer's forehead. But he accidentally turned it into a dark, more noticeable, frown-like smear. Po gulped. That was . . . worse. Much worse.

Master Shifu wiped his head clean.

"We have to talk," he said, seriously.

"Absolutely," Po replied. Since Master Shifu had approached him, there must be a serious situation. But Po was *also* about to be in a serious situation if he didn't get to Mr. Ping's noodle restaurant ASAP. "Let's do that . . . right after the ceremony!"

Po sped off.

At the noodle restaurant, Po held a staff up high in the sky and addressed the crowd.

"The Staff of Wisdom," Po explained. "Given to me by Master Oogway himself. It is said that whoever possesses this staff has the power to travel between the realms, the

8

power to unlock the door to the Spirit Realm. And now, the power to open . . ." Po swung the staff and cut through a ribbon. "The all-new 'Dragon Warrior Noodles and Tofu,' where the broth has *KICK!*"

Po somersaulted into a kick as if to demonstrate the broth's power. The crowd cheered; confetti fell from the sky.

"And the bean curd's a *KNOCKOUT*!" Po slammed his fist onto the ground, sending vibrations across the pavement. Mr. Ping jumped as a stream of confetti fluttered out of a dragon's mouth. The crowd continued cheering.

A horde of kids appeared around Po.

"Will the Furious Five be here, too?" asked a piglet.

The kids all held up their action figures of the Furious Five—a quintet of kung fu warriors: Tigress, Viper, Crane, Monkey, and Mantis.

Po reached down to pose one of the arms on the Tigress action figure.

"Unfortunately, no," Po replied. "They're off on supercool kung fu missions."

Po held one of the kids' Mantis action figures. Just as he moved his hand, the figure's head fell off. He reattached it onto the toy.

"I wish the Furious Five were here," one of the panda cubs lamented.

"Just because they're not here in person doesn't mean they're not here as life-size cutouts!" Po said cheerfully. "Now, who wants a picture?"

Po stood proud while his dads pushed in cardboard cutouts of the Furious Five on both sides of him. A chorus of eager cheers erupted from the kids.

Po hoisted each kid up onto his shoulder as a local pig artist drew a portrait.

"And then you . . ." Po said, posing with another one.

The artist presented the picture to them.

Uh-oh. That portrait didn't have a kid in it at all. It did, however, have Master Shifu.

And Master Shifu was still perched on Po's shoulder. He looked angry.

"The artist really captured your disapproving scowl," said Po sincerely.

"We need to talk," replied Master Shifu. And with that, he hopped down from Po's shoulder. "*Now.*"

Po followed his master, but not before whispering to the artist, "Can I get one of those in a wallet size?"

"Po!" screeched Master Shifu.

"Coming!" said Po, running after him.

CHAPTER 3

Po followed Master Shifu to the Jade Palace. They made their way up the seemingly endless staircase.

"Do you remember the first time you climbed these steps up to the Jade Palace?" asked Master Shifu.

Po was out of breath.

"How could I forget? I thought I'd never make it to the top," he huffed.

"Yes, but you persevered." Master Shifu looked serious. "And, once again, destiny calls for you to take the next step on your journey."

"The next step? What are you talking about? I've already taken all the steps," said Po, confused. He was the Dragon Warrior, after all! "Haven't I?"

"It's time for you to choose your successor."

"Successor? For what?"

"A successor to be the next Dragon Warrior."

"Whoa, whoa, whoa, wait, wait," Po said, concern dawning on his face. "You mean . . . I won't be the Dragon Warrior anymore? Then what am I going to be?"

"Once a successor is chosen, you will advance to the highest level in all of kung fu . . . Spiritual Leader of the Valley of Peace." Master Shifu's voice resonated against the stone steps.

"Whoa," said Po. "I don't know what that means."

They continued up the steps.

"It's just like Master Oogway before you. You will oversee the valley, passing along wisdom and inspiring hope," Master Shifu explained.

Master Oogway had indeed given Po a lot of wisdom and hope. But Po wasn't ready to give up the Dragon Warrior mantle just yet.

"I think I'm just gonna stick with the whole Dragon Warrior thing," Po said.

"Dragon Warrior *thing*?" repeated Master Shifu. "What is it you're holding?"

Po held out a cookie that was in one hand.

Master Shifu was not amused. "*Other hand.*"

"The Staff of Wisdom," answered Po.

"It was given to you by Master Oogway," said Master Shifu. He smacked the cookie away. "Do you really think it was so you could open a restaurant? Or pose for pictures?"

"He wasn't super specific," replied Po.

"Oogway entrusted you with that sacred staff so that you may evolve beyond your true self and transcend to your rightful place in the universe." Master Shifu stood tall and proud as they both reached the top of the steps.

Po shoved the Staff of Wisdom at Master Shifu.

"You take it," he said.

"No," replied Master Shifu. "Oogway did not give it to me. Being the next Oogway is not my destiny. I have accepted it, and I am at peace with it. Really. It's fine."

"You don't sound fine," Po said with a sidelong glance.

"I said I'm fine!"

"Okay, okay, you're fine."

"This is an honor! Oogway chose you as his successor, and now you must choose yours!"

Master Shifu turned to a withered potted tree nearby. Using his chi, he transformed it back into a healthy plant.

"Master Shifu," Po started. "I finally found something I'm good at, and now you want to just take it away from me?"

"No one is taking anything away, Po. Who you are will always be a part of what you become," said Master Shifu.

"Yeah, but where's the *skadoosh*?" Po replied. "You know what I mean? The shasha-booie? I don't want to seem ungrateful, but I don't know anything about passing on wisdom or inspiring hope." Po shrugged. "All I know are two things: kickin' butt and taking names . . . and if I'm being completely honest, I'm not even that good at the name-taking part. Like, who was that fire-breathing crocodile? I want to say Steve . . ."

"You were chosen to bring peace to the valley, and there are other ways to bring peace than simply *kicking butt*," said Master Shifu.

"Well, sure, but not any fun ones. Please," Po continued. "Being the Dragon Warrior is all I know. It's who I am!"

"I'm sorry, but this is your destiny, Po," Master Shifu said seriously. "You'll start interviewing candidates first thing tomorrow morning." With that, he headed into the Hall of Heroes and shut the door behind him, leaving Po all alone. The Hall of Heroes housed some of the most precious and valuable antiquities from the history of kung fu, not to mention an impressive collection of weapons.

"Candidates?" Po said to himself. "What candidates?"

And if Master Shifu was just going to lock him out, why couldn't he have let Po have that cookie?

CHAPTER 4

The "candidates" for Po's successor as Dragon Warrior were at the Jade Palace theater the next morning. Po and Master Shifu sat with a crowd, watching as each candidate demonstrated their skills.

A bull tossed two pieces of fruit into the air, then slashed them into perfectly crafted citrus replicas of Po and Master Shifu. Po still wasn't keen on the idea of a successor, but even he had to admit this was impressive.

A piglet wearing winged armor jumped off the ceiling rafters and soared through multiple hoops.

"No way!" Po exclaimed.

An antelope headbutted a row of bamboo poles, splitting each one in half.

Po chuckled, impressed.

Another pig, wearing pig-friendly paints to look like a panda, stood in a heroic pose, his cape *whooshing* under him. "Skadoosh!" said the panda pig.

"Fantastic pose," Po said to Master Shifu.

A muscular goat picked up a boulder, tossed it into the air, and kicked it into another boulder, smashing it to pieces. Debris flew over the awe-struck crowd. The goat headbutted the last boulder, cracking it in half with his horns.

The crowd cheered. A gong sounded, signaling the end of tryouts.

Master Shifu stood. "Master Po will now choose the next Dragon Warrior!"

"Uh-oh," Po said, more to himself than anyone else. He liked all of these candidates well enough, but he wasn't done being the Dragon Warrior.

TACK. TACK. TACK. A line of drummers rapped their sticks methodically into a warrior anthem, building suspense. The candidates patiently waited. Po wavered his finger back and forth across the line of candidates, all eyes on him. The drumming stopped and Po was expected to make his announcement.

"I've made my choice," Po said finally. The crowd looked on with bated breath. "And it is . . . to not have to choose."

The crowd gasped. Master Shifu jumped to his feet.

"Like it or not, you have to choose a successor," Master Shifu said to Po.

"What can I tell you? You know when you know . . . y'know?" Po said.

"No, *I* don't know. But *you* need to know!" screeched Master Shifu. "Meditate! Ask the universe! Flip a coin! I don't care, but the Valley of Peace needs an answer!"

Outside, Po stood in front of a blossoming peach tree, holding a peach pit in his paw.

"Every pit holds the strength of a mighty tree," he said to himself.

He sat down. He was no good at this "wisdom" stuff. He closed his eyes and prepared to meditate, hoping the universe would offer some guidance.

As Po fell into a meditative state, he kept visualizing himself as multiple floating Po heads.

Inner peace . . . inner peace . . . inner peace . . . dinner please . . . dinner with peas . . . snow peas? . . . In a sesame soy glaze?

His meditation was not working at all.

He chided himself internally.

Maybe focus on your breathing, said Po's inner voice.

I'm trying, but it's kinda hard when you keep talking to me! replied Po.

Technically, you're talking to you, if you think about it, said Po's inner voice.

Hey, will you two be quiet? I'm trying to concentrate here. This was Po's inner, *inner* voice.

How many voices do I have in there? asked Po.

You do not want to know, said another inner, inner voice.

This dirt is itchy.

I just love kung fu.

Are we alone in the universe?

Did you hear my stomach growl?

Helloooo?

What's a successor again?

Did someone mention dinner?

Do any of you guys sing?

Stop copying me!

Okay, wait a minute. Wait! Wait.

A cookie?

"Ahhh!" Po shrieked.

The cacophony of inner Po voices was just too much. He couldn't meditate properly.

All around him, the peach tree petals fell, forming an ethereal yin-yang symbol.

Po accidentally inhaled a petal and gagged. Just as he spit it out, he saw a cloaked figure in the distance. The figure disappeared into a window of the Jade Palace.

Po's eyes narrowed as he watched the figure.

"Huh?" he said.

Meditation would have to wait. He needed to investigate.

Po followed the figure to the Hall of Heroes.

"Attention, mysterious figure!" Po called out. "The Dragon Warrior is here . . . to perform justice!"

High above Po in the rafters of the Hall of Heroes, in the nostril of Master Rhino's statue, a paw silently slipped out. Once uncovered, the paw swung a lasso around the statue's tusk and dropped down.

Before Po could blink, the figure grabbed a Hall of Heroes artifact and retreated back up. Then it did it again, gone before Po could spin around fast enough.

"I know you're in here," Po said, surveying the room. "It's just a matter of time before I find you. Ooo . . ."

Po stopped, distracted by his reflection in a gold plate. Then, since his back was itchy, he scratched it with the Staff of Wisdom.

Unbeknownst to Po, the mysterious thief had attached herself to Po's back. She winced, dodging the sharp staff. Then she grabbed the gold plate.

"You can't hide from justice forever!" Po called out to the thief.

Po swung the Staff of Wisdom around, performing epic kung fu moves as he jabbed. Then—**WHOOSH!**—the thief's shadowy figure swooped by.

In the reflection of Master Oogway's perfectly pristine statue, Po saw the thief approach a dagger. She was a gray Chinese corsac fox, and Po could tell that she would be a formidable foe.

The fox gripped the dagger's handle and picked it up. Po knew it to be the Dagger of Den Wa.

"You've got excellent taste. But I can't give you that. Give it back," Po said to the fox.

"If you insist," the fox growled.

ZING! The fox hurled the dagger toward Po in an attack. But Po maneuvered the blade upward and cast it toward the ground, blade side crashing down first.

"Huh?" Po screeched as he narrowly dodged the falling dagger. "Handle first would have been nice."

The fox eyed Po's Staff of Wisdom. "Oh no! He's got a walking stick. What are you going to do? Stroll me to death?"

"This stick is not for strolling. It's the Staff of Wisdom," Po replied, offended.

"Did you swipe it off of the Dragon Warrior?" the fox asked sarcastically.

"I *am* the Dragon Warrior," said Po.

The fox eyed Po suspiciously. "I'm just gonna say it. Nothing about you says 'dragon' or 'warrior.'"

Po let out a battle cry and charged at the fox. She bolted out of reach, grabbed two oil lamps, and scaled the figure of Master Rhino. Her hood flew off and Po saw her uncovered face for the first time.

Cornered, the fox threw the oil lamp at the ground, spilling oil all over the floor.

"How dare you desecrate the Hall of Herooooooes—" Po rushed forward to grab her, but he slipped in the oil.

"Who's desecrating what now?" the fox replied with a hint of sarcasm.

Now on top of a pillar, the fox kicked an egg high into the air.

"Master Ostrich Egg!" Po screamed. He ran after the egg, catching it before it hit the ground.

"Oops. My bad," said the fox sarcastically. She flipped over to the next pillar and thew a chain hammer.

"The Indestructible Chain Hammer of Master Pangolin,"

Po cried in horror. The hammer's chains wrapped around his wrists; he was still holding the egg.

"Whoopsies!" said the fox. She then shoved a long row of pedestals around, all holding precious artifacts. With the egg still in his grasp, Po dove for the treasures, skillfully kicking all of them back into the air. Before they plummeted to the ground, Po caught all the artifacts; the last one, an old scroll, landed in his mouth.

The fox approached a delicate-looking urn. She poked it, which caused it to teeter dangerously.

Po spat out the scroll. "The Urn of Whispering Warriors! Which I've already broken . . . twice!"

"Why would you keep an urn of souls? Feels kinda creepy," the fox replied. With a casual swipe of her tail, the urn teetered off the pedestal. Po dove to the urn's rescue, barely saving it before it hit the ground.

Po sighed in relief. But the fight was not yet over.

The fox jumped onto Po's back. "Are you doing okay there, big guy? You're lookin' a little tired."

"I've never felt more awake!" Po said, kicking her off. The fox sailed through the air, slamming into another pedestal, which sent the object atop it flying.

"The Warhammer of Master Chipmunk!" cried Po.

The warhammer hit the urn with a delicate *tink!* The

urn shattered and released a pile of ashes. The souls released from the urn cried out in agony.

"You're gonna pay for that. And the guy that repairs these things charges a fortune," Po told the fox.

But the fox was still lying on the floor of the hall, seemingly knocked out from being thrown headlong into the pedestal. Po went over to her.

"Hello?" Po said, gingerly poking the fox with his staff.

The fox's eyes snapped open and her lips curled into a deceitful smile. It had been a ruse! She kicked Po. Po's staff flew out of his hand as he slid back into the pile of ashes. The souls once again cried out in agony.

"You faker!" said Po indignantly.

The fox caught the staff, gave it a twirl, and walked toward the exit.

"It's not faking. It's called *method*. Catch ya later, panda!" she called.

Po rose from the pool of oil, slipping and sliding ungracefully as he did.

"No, I think I'll catch you now!" he yelled after her.

Po assumed a fighting stance. Two pillars flew past the fox and slammed the door shut in front of her. As she turned around, Po hurled two more pillars at the exit, barricading her inside. Then, the final pillars careened toward her. They spun through the air, revealing The Indestructible Chain Hammer of Master Pangolin fastened between them. The fox gasped and ducked out of the way.

"Whoaaaaa," the fox said.

She tightened her grip on the staff, refusing to let go. But it was no use. The chains wrapped around her. She was caught! Po slipped the Staff of Wisdom out of her hands.

"Told ya," Po said. He felt triumphant.

"You got me, oh great and powerful Dumpling Warrior," the fox retorted.

"That's *Dragon* Warrior!"

CHAPTER 5

Po locked the fox in a jail cart. Soon, it would take her away to the Valley of Peace Prison. But as the barred doors slammed shut, she had just one question.

"How'd you catch me?"

"That's a mystery for you to solve during your two-year stay at the Valley of Peace Prison," Po replied.

"Valley of Peace Prison? Pff. Sounds like a daycare."

"It *is* a daycare on the weekends," he said. He leaned in close. "But it's also a prison."

Just then, there was commotion in the town square. Po and the fox looked up curiously. A herd of ram miners were running toward Po.

"There he is!" said one of the rams. It was the supervisor.

The rams stopped in front of Po and the fox. "Tai Lung is back!" They looked panicked.

"He demanded all of our iron, then destroyed our quarry!"

None of that made sense to Po. Tai Lung had been defeated. Po made sure of that, many moons ago.

"He's supposed to be in the Spirit Realm," Po reminded the rams. "You know, permanently."

"Well, he's back," piped one of the rams.

"He said that he's not going to stop until the Valley of Peace falls and the Dragon Warrior bows before him," added the supervisor. The miners murmured among themselves.

"Tai Lung has returned? But how?" Po mused out loud. As he mulled over this, the fox's jail cart rolled past him.

"Hmm. Looks like I'm not the only one around here with a mystery to solve," she said. The cart rolled away further. "Well, you know what they say: every step leaves a footprint, no matter how small." With that, the fox was carted away.

Po's distraught gaze fell upon the distant mountain top. If Tai Lung had re-emerged, he would have to investigate.

Po left quickly. At dusk, he reached the quarry. As he walked through it, he noted that the iron mine was crumbling, abandoned hastily by the frightened miners.

Po's lantern illuminated a set of snow leopard tracks that

led into the mine shaft, and an uneasy feeling settled on him. He knew immediately to whom those tracks belonged. The snow leopard was Tai Lung.

"Every step leaves a footprint," Po said to himself, following the tracks. They grew ever smaller until eventually they were tiny reptilian-like prints. "No matter how small."

Po thought about the mysterious fox, and how those were her parting words.

The fox knew something.

Po was intent on finding out what.

Po left the quarry and ventured to the fox's jail cell in the Valley of Peace Prison.

"Very clever, fox. You know something," he said to her.

"Maybe I do. Maybe I don't," the fox replied. There was a beat of silence. But then she jumped up, unable to hide her excitement. "Okay, I do. I really, really do!"

"Tell me," instructed Po.

"And why should I? I mean, what's in it for me?"

"The peace of mind knowing you did the right thing."

The fox sneered. "You're adorable. Has anyone ever told you that?"

"I don't have time for games," Po said. "Tai Lung is running loose in the Valley of Peace."

"Maybe . . . or maybe she *wants* you to think it was Tai Lung," said the fox. She launched into a story.

The Empress of Disguise was a villain capable of mimicking any shape or form—a chameleon, a bull, a crocodile, a bear, a rhino—even Tai Lung.

"She can manipulate anyone into giving her anything she wants," the fox continued.

The Empress of Disguise, the fox explained, was also known as The Chameleon.

Upon hearing the name, the geese guards gasped. They clearly were eavesdropping.

"This is kind of a private conversation," Po said to them. The geese guards walked off.

Po turned back to the fox. "Who's The Chameleon?"

"Only the world's most powerful shapeshifting sorceress," said the fox, as though it should be obvious. "She isn't someone who can be found. At least not without someone in the know."

"And how do I find someone 'in the know'?"

Po was prepared to do whatever it took to find Tai Lung—or the Tai Lung impostor. He couldn't imagine what kind of havoc they could wreak.

The fox twitched.

"Aghh, it's me. It's obviously me. I'm in the—I mean—I'm in the know."

Po was disappointed. He was prepared to do whatever it took, *except* for team up with this sneaky fox.

"Forget it! I'll find her on my own," Po muttered.

"Good luck!" called the fox from behind her cell bars. "After all, how hard can it be to find someone who can look like anyone, blend in anywhere. . . ."

Po stopped in his tracks and slowly walked back to the jail cell. He hated to admit it, but the fox was right. He'd have to work with her if he wanted to stop this dangerous threat.

"Fine. You lead me to The Chameleon, and I'll see what I can do about reducing your sentence."

"Deal!" the fox said. She bowed and Po returned the honorable gesture.

"Po!" rang out a sudden voice. "What do you think you're doing?"

Po turned around to see Master Shifu, looming in the doorway with the two geese guards by his side.

"Uh, there's this shapeshifting sorceress on the loose and—"

"That's a job for the Furious Five," Master Shifu cut in. "Your job is finding a successor."

"The Dragon Warrior and I have a deal. Mind your own business, squirrel," the fox interjected.

Po was shocked. Sure, Master Shifu could be a bit, well . . . *disciplined*, but this fox was downright rude!

"Master Shifu is not a squirrel," Po said.

"I'm a red panda," replied Master Shifu.

"You know what? I love that for you," the fox joked.

Master Shifu ignored the fox. "Po, this is your decision, but I think you know what choice Master Oogway would want you to make."

Po composed himself. Master Shifu was right—he knew what Master Oogway would want Po to do. He'd want Po to honor his promises. Now, that promise included Po's deal with the fox.

Seconds later, the fox rushed outside the prison's main door, wedging a guard in the door's window. She shook the goose's wing.

"Thanks for the free stay!"

"Wait!" Master Shifu cried.

"Don't worry," Po assured him. "I'll have her back before you even know she was gone."

"You are supposed to be passing along wisdom and inspiring hope!" Master Shifu called out to Po.

"Just think of it as one last Dragon Warrior adventure.

I'll be back soon. Tell my dads I love 'em. I can't hear you anymore! Byeeeeee!"

Po and the fox disappeared over the horizon.

Master Shifu was furious. Po had shirked his duties *and* ignored him.

CHAPTER 6

The next morning, Po and the fox, who Po learned was named Zhen, were walking through the countryside. Zhen ran excitedly around Po, bouncing off the nearby rocks and branches. Po marched onward, annoyed by her energetic bursts.

"Yeah! It sure is good to be a free fox again!" she said.

"You were in jail for less than a day," Po reminded her.

Zhen gave him a look of mocking regret. "And boy, have I learned my lesson!"

She jumped over Po's shoulder and grabbed the Staff of Wisdom from him.

"So, does this really unlock the door to the Spirit Realm?" Zhen asked. She waved the Staff of Wisdom around. "Shazar! Skablam!"

Po grabbed the staff. "It doesn't work like that," he said curtly. "It has to be given in order to gain its powers."

"Gotcha," she said, nodding. "Given to gain. So, um, can I have it?"

"No! What do you take me for?"

"An easy mark." Zhen shrugged.

"What's an easy mark?"

"Someone who's easy to steal from. Usually because they're generous and too trusting. Like you."

Po scoffed. He didn't think he was too trusting.

Meanwhile, back at the newly crowned Dragon Warrior Noodles and Tofu, Mr. Ping and Li were bustling around the busy restaurant. The crowd was abuzz with rumors of the mysterious and menacing threat . . . The Chameleon.

How did they hear about this newest foe? Well, sitting at one of the restaurant's tables was a goose guard from the Valley of Peace prison.

"*I* heard The Chameleon is a monster with an appetite of a thousand predators! And her favorite food is panda," the guard said dramatically.

At another table sat a fluffle of bunnies and an old rabbit.

"If you say her name three times, she'll take you away in the night!" The old rabbit said, spinning a tale. The bunnies gasped as Li cleared away their dishes.

"The Chameleon can shapeshift to look like anyone. Even you!" said a pig at the next table.

The rumors continued to fly.

"Mr. Li! Mr. Li! Is it true?" said one of the bunnies.

"Po's gonna take down an evil sorceress?" another bunny finished the thought.

Another bunny popped out of a bowl Li was holding. "*The* Chameleon?"

Li laughed heartily. "Well, a Dragon Warrior's work is never done."

Li headed back into the kitchen where a concerned Mr. Ping was chopping carrots. Clearly, Mr. Ping wasn't taking the "Chameleon Business" as lightly as Li.

"I'm thinking Po's decision to team up with a convicted felon to take down an evil sorceress wasn't such a great idea," Mr. Ping said.

Li took a bite of food. "Relax. Po has faced demons, demi-gods, and everything else in between. He's always come out on top." His words were true, of course. Po had indeed faced many foes before. Li picked up several bowls of noodles and balanced them expertly in his arms.

"Ah, you're right, you're right," Mr. Ping replied.

He was reassured for a second, but one second only. Then another thought came to him.

"But what if you're wrong?"

CHAPTER 7

Four fancily dressed Komodo dragon guards carried a tiny, robed figure—The Chameleon—into a courtyard. Five crime bosses—Bear, Croc, Boar, Badger, and Wolf—were already gathered around a table, waiting for her.

"Sorry to have kept you waiting," The Chameleon said to them. "And by 'sorry,' I mean 'not really.'"

The Komodo dragon guards placed a miniature tea set in front of each of the crime bosses. Bear looked down at the tiny portion and growled. The teacup may have been suitable for a chameleon, but it was hardly anything for a large bear.

"Due to the expansion of my ever-growing empire, I'm going to have to raise your weekly tributes. Again," The Chameleon announced.

Wolf had just taken a sip from her tiny teacup, but upon hearing this news, she spat out her tea. The crime bosses' weekly tributes to The Chameleon were funds they'd never see again. Badger moved some beads over on his abacus, calculating what this new rate would cost him.

"Raising them to what?" Wolf asked, trying to keep her composure.

"Fifty-five percent," replied The Chameleon.

"But we already agreed on fifty!"

"Did I say fifty-five?" The Chameleon taunted. "I meant sixty." She wanted to demonstrate what talking back to her cost. (Five percent more.)

"No," Bear said curtly.

The other bosses gasped.

"What was that now?" The Chameleon sneered.

"I said no," Bear replied. Then he threw his tiny teacup. **CRASH!** It pummeled into one of the guards' faces, but the guard remained unfazed. "You may have everyone else at this table fooled with your tough talk and magic tricks, but not me. You're nothing but a cold-blooded fraud!" Bear slammed an axe on the table, creating a menacing crack that spread all the way to The Chameleon's feet.

The Chameleon, however, was unbothered. She picked up a fallen tea kettle and refilled Wolf's cup.

"You know, when I first arrived here, I dreamed that one day I was going to rule Juniper City. It wasn't easy. I was overlooked. Underestimated. But thanks to hard work, dedication, and a little old-fashioned *magic*—" The Chameleon's eyes glowed. "My dream has finally come true. And by this time tomorrow, I will expand my reign beyond, to every valley and village across the land. Which brings me to the elephant in the room . . ."

The Chameleon's eyes grew brighter as she took the form of a massive, terrifying elephant. She squished the table as she grew, sending crime bosses flying. Then she grabbed Bear with her trunk and lifted him up to face her.

"If anyone dares question my authority again, I'll show that I'm not the only one around here who can turn into something ugly. Am I making myself clear?"

Bear nodded nervously.

"Crystal."

Just to be sure, The Chameleon demonstrated some of her power. She thrashed Bear around and threw him onto the other crime bosses. "I'll expect each of your tributes by the end of the week. Ta-ta."

With that, the crime bosses scrambled away.

The Chameleon transformed back into her original form. She caught her reflection in the bear's axe.

"I think that went well," she said to herself.

"Very well!" replied one of the guards.

"I'd say!" chimed another.

The Chameleon rolled her eyes. It had been a *rhetorical* comment. On her glare, the two guards whimpered and quickly went back to cleaning the mess.

The Chameleon studied her reflection again.

CHAPTER 8

Zhen and Po made their way through a bright green bamboo forest.

"How did you even become the Dragon Warrior?" Zhen asked Po.

"When I looked into the Dragon Scroll, I saw my own reflection," Po replied. "And that's when I realized that the secret to limitless power was me."

"So, what you're saying is, you became the Dragon Warrior because you looked into a mirror and . . . saw yourself," said Zhen.

"Well, it sounds way less cool when you say it like that."

They continued their journey and eventually came to a big rock gully, where a powerful river crashed against the bluffs below. Zhen easily hopped around, but Po struggled. He landed in the splits between the two cliffs.

"And you're really not worried about going up against the world's most powerful sorceress?"

"Please," Po said confidently. "I eat powerful sorceresses for breakfast. Well, actually congee, usually . . . but, uh, powerful sorceresses for my mid-morning snack."

As they talked, Po found it difficult to make his way around the cliff.

"And after you find The Chameleon, the plan is . . . .?"

"To kick Chameleon butt, make her give back everything she stole, and learn from the error of her ways. So, how much farther is it to this The Chameleon?" Po said, still trying to gain some footing.

"Just a little further," Zhen promised.

They made it through a water ridge, an arid plain, a rice patty pond, a prairie bridge, some waterfalls, and a large, edgy cliff.

"Little farther," Zhen promised each time.

Po, finally pushed to his limit, threw off his backpack.

"That's it! I'm not taking another step until you tell me where we're going," he demanded.

"If you want to know where we're going, then why don't you just turn around and take a look?"

Po's eyes widened. Off in the distance was a vast, brimming metropolis surrounded by water.

"Whoa, that's the biggest village I've ever seen," he said.

"That's no village," said Zhen. "That's Juniper City."

"That's where I'll find The Chameleon, huh?"

"Just a boat ride away," she replied. "And—as promised—I'm going to lead you right to her front door."

Po eyed Juniper City with determination.

He hoped The Chameleon was ready to meet her match.

Mr. Ping had packed his travel bag and scurried out of the noodle restaurant, hoping no one would notice his silhouette sneaking out in the night. Just when he thought he'd gotten away with it, none other than Li wiggled himself over the restaurant's roof and slid off—**CRASH!** He landed directly in front of Mr. Ping.

"AH!!!" screamed Mr. Ping.

"AH!!!" screamed Li.

"AH!!!" screamed Mr. Ping.

"AH!!!" screamed Li.

"AH!!!" screamed Mr. Ping.

"AH!!!" screamed Li.

"Oooo!" said Mr. Ping.

"AH!" said Li.

"What are you doing out here in the middle of the night?" Mr. Ping asked.

Li stood up and dusted himself off. "I—I didn't want to miss the blood moon rising," he said sheepishly.

"Oh, poo. You are just as worried as I am," said Mr. Ping knowingly.

Li relented. "Alright, alright. I know pandas come across as calm, gentle, and chill, but the truth is . . . *I'm kinda freaking out!*"

"So am I! Po is just too calm, gentle, and chill to face a shapeshifting sorceress."

"What if he's captured?" said Li, worry riddled across his panda face.

"What if he's tortured?" mused Mr. Ping.

They both gasped at the same time.

"OUR BABY!"

Mr. Ping took a moment to compose himself. "Okay, okay, maybe Po has finally met his match, but there is still something that he has that The Chameleon does not."

"What's that?" Li asked.

"*Us,*" said Mr. Ping with confidence. "Now, let's go find our son!"

Li appreciated the confidence, but he was still worried.

"I hope Po's okay," Li said.

Mr. Ping put a consoling wing around him.

"You know, Li, a wise goose once said, 'Worrying doesn't make the broth boil any faster.'"

"Who said that?"

"Me, of course! I was the wise goose."

And with that, the two dads hurried off in pursuit of Po—together.

CHAPTER 9

Po and Zhen headed toward a tavern. They were on a mission to find a boat—and a captain—who would take them to Juniper City. Po believed that, for the right price, a captain would take them anywhere they wanted to go. Zhen believed that they could always do the good ol' four-finger discount, but Po didn't condone stealing.

"C'mon! You're the Dragon Warrior," Zhen said. "Why don't you just walk in there and lay the smack down on these jokers until they give us what we want?"

"A kung fu master only uses physical violence as a last resort," Po replied simply.

They neared the front door of a tavern.

A rusty sign that read "THE HAPPY BUNNY TAVERN" swung in the gentle sea breeze, creaking back and forth.

Just then—**SMASH!**—the front door exploded open. A disheveled bunny slammed into them and bounced off Po's belly. The bunny screamed.

Po stepped inside the door and held the bunny up. "Anybody lose a rabbit?"

The inside of the tavern was packed with patrons drinking, gambling, and disrespecting the waitstaff, all of which were bunnies.

In the kitchen, a bunny sat inside a steaming pot, stirring the contents. Granny Boar—the fine establishment's chef—added some spices to the pot, which sent steam into the air. The bunny whimpered.

"Stir faster," Granny Boar demanded.

The bunny in Po's grasp turned to him. "Welcome to the Happy Bunny Tavern."

Po set down the bunny. **THWACK!** A large axe from one of the tavern's patrons barreled into the wall behind them. Unfazed, Po hung his hat on the edge of the axe blade and turned to face Zhen.

"I'll find us a ride. Maybe you can get us some food. And stay out of trouble."

Po headed off on his mission. As instructed, Zhen walked up to a table.

"Whatchu guys playin'?" she asked.

"Mahjong," Granny Boar grunted. She jumped on the table and captured a twirling mahjong tile. "And the stakes are high."

"Can I play? Surely you'll go easy on a beginner. . . ." Zhen batted her eyes.

The patrons around the table grinned and chuckled.

Meanwhile, Po approached a bunny server.

"What can I get you?" the server asked Po.

"Uh, a boat ride to Juniper City."

"Ask this guy . . ." the server said, motioning to a pelican.

"Who's he?" asked Po.

"He's the captain," replied the server.

"Thanks." Po dropped a coin into the tip jar on top of the wood counter. As he walked away, a wolf swiped the tip out of the jar. The bunny server sighed softly and went back to his work.

Po sat next to the pelican and learned his name was Chip.

"I can give you a ride. You bringing anything illegal? 'Cuz I don't want any trouble," Chip said. His voice seemed muffled, but Po wasn't sure why.

"Trouble runs from me," Po assured him.

"Then it'll cost you double," Chip replied.

Po was confused. "Should I have said that I *like* trouble?"

"In that case, it'll cost you triple!"

"Oh, uh . . . maybe we can go back to the double price?" Po asked. He reached into his pocket, pulled out a bag of coins, and showed it to Chip. A tiny sword popped out of Chip's mouth and sliced through the money bag. Then, a small fish—aptly named Fish—leaned out of Chip's mouth and looked at the treasure.

"You got a deal," said Fish, revealing that he was speaking for Chip the whole time.

"Great!" Po said. "Do I shake his hand or your hand?" Po chuckled.

CHAPTER 10

Meanwhile, at the mahjong table, Zhen piled the coins in front of her.

"Oh, I win again. Beginner's luck, I guess."

"Never played before, huh?" Granny Boar asked suspiciously.

"I'm sorry," Zhen said, mocking offense with a smile. "Are you accusing me of cheating? I would like to speak to the manager, please."

"I am the manager," Granny Boar replied.

"Oh. In that case, I'd like a menu and three of your favorite starters. Hehe."

Granny Boar growled but brought over the menu.

Soon, Zhen was seated in front of a huge feast.

"Can I get anything else for you, ma'am?" asked one of the bunny waiters.

"Yes, everything again except for the broth. It was very bland," she replied.

Po arrived at the table.

"Whoa," he said, eyeing the feast. "One of everything is my go-to order! But how did you pay for this?"

"Legally. Lawfully. Fair and square," Zhen assured him.

"Aw, I'm proud of you."

As Po said that, Zhen moved too abruptly and an avalanche of mahjong tiles poured out from her tail. The entire tavern gasped as the final tile piece fell to the floor. "Fair and square" their butts—Zhen had cheated! Granny Boar growled menacingly and her henchmen appeared, weapons at the ready.

Zhen jumped up quickly. She grabbed Po's hand and led him away from the table. "Oh, wow, look at the time! Remember we have to do that thing down by the place with that guy?"

But Granny Boar and the tavern patrons were not pleased. They blocked their path.

"Did you actually think you could grift a meal out of me?" Granny Boar sneered.

Po tried to defuse the situation. "There's gotta be some

sort of misunderstanding here." He cast a sidelong glance at Zhen, but aside from looking apologetic, she offered no explanation.

Po sighed. Clearly, he was the one who had misunderstood. "Please, allow us to pay for our meal and yours, too."

Granny Boar looked at the pair. "I'm only hungry for—"

"Dumplings?" suggested Po.

"Vengeance!" Granny finished.

"Well, then . . . *come and get it*," Zhen teased, bringing the situation to a boil.

"No, n-n-n-no. Don't come and get it!" Po begged uselessly, but it was too late.

"Destroy them!" Granny Boar shouted.

Zhen smacked a group of patrons out of the way and ran. Po wielded the Staff of Wisdom to fling some of Granny Boar's henchmen against the wall. The impact of the blow broke one of the tavern's support beams and the whole building tilted to the side. It was pure chaos! Henchmen lost their balance and jostled around the tavern, a pig flew and crashed to the side, and Fish tumbled out of Chip's mouth toward an open flame.

"AHHHH!" Fish screamed.

Po caught the fish before he was barbecued and placed him safely back with Chip.

Zhen pounced onto the bar. She dodged a sword and kicked a henchman into a group of patrons. They barreled into a side wall, and the building teetered, this time in the opposite direction. The crowd lost their balance yet again.

Po saved some bunnies from being further bullied by the henchmen and fended off a slew of angry tavern-goers.

"Whoa!" said Po. "Gotcha."

Zhen continued fighting off members of Granny Boar's crew atop a nearby table. She kicked over a bowl of chili flakes into the wolf's eyes. (Don't try that at home.) Covered in spice, the wolf howled in pain.

A boar jumped on the other end of the broken table and launched Zhen up to the second floor of the tavern. She landed up top with a great, big *THUMP!*

Po watched as his companion ran across the second floor, taking down opponent after opponent. But he couldn't watch for long. A boar challenged Po to a fight. Po jumped to one side of the tavern, causing it to tilt anew. The boar lost his balance and slid away.

On the second floor, Zhen was now engaged in a fierce battle with the wolf. She dodged blow after blow and eventually hid behind Po. The wolf swung down, but Po blocked his attack with his staff.

Not one to miss an opportunity, Zhen hurried over and

stole money from the boar's bag.

"I'll take that," she said, satisfied.

Po grabbed her with his staff. What about the whole "no stealing" thing did Zhen not understand? He shook her up and down, which loosened the pilfered money from her tail. The coins spilled out of her grasp as he released her.

The wolf swung at Po. Po blocked the attack.

A pack of henchmen ascended the stairs. Zhen, perched at the top, pushed barrels toward them, which sent her opponents careening back down to the first floor. In the ensuing chaos, she hopped atop a barrel lid and rode it down the staircase like a skateboard, all the while stealing several patrons' money.

"Hee-yah!" she screeched.

Po followed after her. He swung down from the second floor using a rope.

"Yah!" he cried.

He lassoed Zhen with the rope and spun her around. Then Po started returning the pilfered bags of money.

"Ahhhh!" Zhen screeched once she saw what Po was doing. "I think it's a little too late for that."

"It's never too late to do the right thing," Po told her.

Just then, a wolf from the second floor let out a howl and raced toward Zhen and Po. It was a fearsome attack, so

Po unleashed his Dragon Warrior skills, twirling his staff around and sending the wolf flying.

"*Skadoosh*!" Po cried triumphantly.

The wolf landed against the railing. The tavern tilted once again.

Zhen admired Po's kung fu prowess. "Nice move," she said. "You gotta teach me that sometime."

But they weren't done yet. Granny Boar stepped forward. She removed her tusks, wielded them like knives, and roared.

Granny Boar was nimble and agile; she matched Po blow for blow as he fought back. Then, she used her tusks to launch Po toward Zhen, who was busy stashing some more looted gold. Po tumbled into her when suddenly—

BOOM!!!

Po and Zhen burst out the side of the lopsided tavern, right to the edge of the cliff, where the tavern's backyard met a watery abyss. Po's staff caught on one piece of the tavern's broken railing, and he clung on for dear life. His cape, however, was not as lucky. It detached from his body and fell into the murky water.

Po reached out lightning fast to grab Zhen's tail before she, too, careened into the water. Their combined weight on the broken railing pulled the tavern even more off-kilter.

"Ahhh!" screamed Zhen. "Whoa, whoa, whoa! Who designs a tavern on a cliff?"

Po tried to console her. "We're okay. It'll be fine," he said. But then his grip loosened. "Uh-oh."

Po and Zhen screamed as they plunged downward.

CHAPTER 11

"**A**HHHH!" Po and Zhen yelled at the same time. They were done for. Goners. This was the end.

Or was it?

CRASH! Somehow, miraculously, the pair landed on the deck of Fish and Chip's boat. Chip immediately cut the line to open the sail.

"Sail ho!" Fish yelled as they made a speedy getaway.

Fish and Chip turned to Po. "Hey, hey, hey, if you're bringing the fox with you, it's gonna cost ya extra."

"Excuse you," Zhen said. "I'm a thief, not a freeloader. Compliments of this guy's smackdown." She pulled a pilfered coin purse out from her tail and handed it to Chip.

Fish inspected it.

"That'll cover it," he said at last.

Po groaned. They made a getaway, sure, but he'd failed at teaching Zhen that stealing was wrong.

The boat sailed into the night.

Mr. Ping and Li trekked through the countryside. Mr. Ping sang Chinese opera as he walked.

"Ping," said Li.

Mr. Ping continued singing.

"Ping," repeated Li, his annoyance mounting.

Mr. Ping continued singing.

"Ping! Will you please just relax?"

Mr. Ping stopped. "Well, I'm worried about Po. And I sing opera when I'm worried."

"You know, a wise goose once told me, 'Worrying doesn't make the broth boil any quicker,'" Li reminded him.

"Sometimes, a wise goose just can't help himself and he worries," replied Mr. Ping.

Li nodded. "Well . . . why don't we take turns worrying?"

Mr. Ping smiled. That seemed like a good idea.

"You can have the next thirty miles, and I'll take what's leftover until we find Po," Mr. Ping said.

"Yeah . . . that seems like a fair trade," Li replied.

The two continued on. Mr. Ping sang his opera again.
"Ping!"

* * 🏮 * *

Fish and Chip's sailboat cut through a foggy, wide-mouthed river. Po and Zhen took this moment of downtime to do some training. They sparred on the deck—Po wielding his staff, Zhen fighting with a broom.

"Twirl! Strike! Spin! Strike! *SKA-BLAM!*" Zhen yelled out the moves as she did them.

"Okay, not bad," said Po. "But it's *fake* and then *strike*. Oh, and it's *skadoosh*."

"Skadoosh isn't a word."

"And ska-blam is?" Po asked.

Fish groaned from the other side of the deck.

Zhen clambered up the edge of the boat and looked at the moonlit horizon through the low fog. The stars flickered overhead.

"I can't wait to show off my new moves when I get to the city," she said excitedly.

"Does your family live there, too?" Po asked. He realized that he hadn't asked Zhen much about herself.

"They would, if I had a family."

"Whoa," said Po. "You're an orphan? So am I! Well, I mean, I was. Now I have two dads. So, when you were growing up, how did you—?"

"—survive? Any way I could. Grifting, shilling, gaffing. . . ."

"I don't know any of those words," admitted Po.

"One day, a local took me in, put a roof over my head, gave me clothes to wear, food to eat . . . . After that, I was never alone again." Zhen hopped down from the boat's edge. "By the way, what did that angry squirrel mean when he said you had to find your successor?"

Oh, right. Master Shifu and the whole "Dragon Warrior successor" thing. In the hubbub, Po had almost forgotten.

"Well, now that I've been promoted to Spiritual Leader, I have to find a worthy successor to take over as the Dragon Warrior," explained Po. "But becoming the Dragon Warrior was my destiny. What do I know about being a Spiritual Leader? I can't even come up with one of those cool-sounding proverbs." He tried to muster something. "Life's greatest enemy is—ugh, I don't know, uh, stairs?"

At the helm, Fish grumbled again.

Po continued. "Sometimes, I wish Master Oogway never even gave me this staff . . ."

"I guess it's just easier to hold on to the life you know than move on to the one you don't," said Zhen.

Po was impressed.

"That was pretty good. Maybe you should be the Spiritual Leader of the Valley of Peace."

"What's it pay?"

Po rolled his eyes. "Yeah, forget about it," he said. "Okay, let's try this again."

They went back to sparring.

"Twirl! Strike! Spin! Strike! *Ska-BLAM!*"

The ship faded into the distance.

"Again, the word is *skadoosh*."

"Again, not a word."

CHAPTER 12

A hot ball of liquid rolled down onto a metal surface in The Chameleon's fortress. **SLAM!** Hammers came down by the dozen. Sparks flew as raw iron ore was smelted and cast into magical cages carved with glyphs.

The Chameleon, flanked by her Komodo dragon guards, moved carefully through her fortress. She was inspecting their progress.

"Iron ore," she noted, examining the mysterious liquid. "Well, at least the Valley of Peace is good for something."

"The spicy tofu?" chirped one of the guards.

"No!" The Chameleon snapped. She used her tongue to choke him for speaking out of turn. Then she continued her thought. "What I admire about iron is its strength. Its endurance. Its *durability*. Iron never weakens. And, after tonight, neither will I." Her eyes glowed. The symbols and glyphs on all the cages lit up.

Meanwhile, Fish and Chip's boat continued sailing down the river. It was now morning, and Po's snores cut through the quiet.

Zhen tried to wake Po up. She fiddled with his ears and mouth and stuck her fingers in his nose. "Wake up, wake up, wake up, wake up, wake up, wake up, wake up, wake up, wake up!"

"Alright!" Po yelped, finally roused.

Zhen pulled Po to the edge of the boat. "We're here," she said excitedly.

Po's morning grogginess faded as the boat passed through a huge city gate. Po stared up in amazement.

"Welcome to Juniper City," said Zhen, as if mimicking a tour guide at a theme park. "Where you can be whatever you wanna be, do whatever you wanna do, and steal whatever you wanna steal."

Indeed, Juniper City was grand and beautiful.

"Land ho," Fish intoned.

The boat approached the dock, and a pig helped guide them to a stop. But instead of slowing down, the boat continued full speed ahead and crashed directly into the dock. The pig ran off, screaming.

"That dock came out of nowhere," said Fish.

Once they were safely docked and debarked, Po and Zhen bid adieu to Fish and Chip and walked through the streets of Juniper City.

One thing was for sure—the city was *bustling*.

Po stood there wide-eyed, mouth agape, as he took everything in.

The Juniper City citizens, however, didn't have time for misty-eyed tourists.

"Comin' through," one citizen said.

"Move!"

"Watch it!"

"Hey!"

"Out of the way!"

Po replied to each of them as more citizens jostled him. "Ugh! Whoa! Oof! Sorry!" He felt a bit like a fish-out-of-water. Po and Zhen missed a couple riding in a carriage.

"I've never seen so much traffic before," Po said.

"What? You don't have 'rush hour' in the Valley of Peace?" asked Zhen.

She continued moving with ease; she was an expert at navigating the humming city. A traffic control goose waved a green and red flag, signaling it was safe to cross.

Po shrugged. No one was ever in that much of a hurry in the Valley of Peace. Po bumped into another citizen. "Oof!" he muttered.

Zhen had already crossed the street. "Come on!"

Finally, Po made it to Zhen's side.

The pair passed by every type of food imaginable. Noodles, rice, dumplings, tofu—Po stared (and sniffed) in amazement.

"Well, it sure is good to be home again," Zhen said. "The sights . . . the sounds—"

Zhen bumped suddenly into Po, who had stopped abruptly to get a whiff of all the food.

"—the smells! Ooooooh," he finished for her.

Po was in a trance from the aroma. He looked in every direction and saw delicious foods of all shapes and sizes. Po admired dish after dish, drooling from the options. He was overwhelmed. Without much thought, he poked his face through a window, accidentally scaring unsuspecting diners. "It's a wonton wonderland!" he called out. Yeah!"

"Po. Focus!" chided Zhen.

"This is the most amazing place I've ever seen," said Po.

"Yeah, I used to feel the same way . . . that is, until The Chameleon got her claws into it."

At that, two Komodo dragon guards from The Chameleon's fortress walked by. Zhen held Po back against the wall to hide. "Let's keep moving," she whispered.

As Zhen and Po made their way through the city, the Juniper City residents called out to Zhen.

"Heya, Zhen!"

"Long time no see!"

"How you doin', Zhen?"

Po cast her a look. "Wow, you're quite the local celebrity," he said.

"Yeah, well, let's just say in this city, a face like mine is hard to forget."

She wasn't wrong. Po saw there was a "WANTED" poster with her face on it right by them.

"*You're a wanted criminal?!*" he cried. They rounded a corner and were suddenly confronted with dozens of wanted posters, all of them plastered with Zhen's coy smile. Zhen leaned up against the wall, unfazed by the posters.

"You sound surprised," she said. "Is this surprising? I don't think this is surprising."

"You never mentioned that you were *wanted*," he hissed back at her.

"Don't worry. The law has better things to do than look for me."

But Zhen was wrong. Two bull police officers appeared just around the corner.

"Hey, fox!" one of the officers called out. "We've been lookin' for you."

"Must be a slow week," Zhen said, sheepish.

The two officers headed toward them.

Po put up his paw as if to say, "I'll handle this."

"Morning, officers! Allow me to introduce myself. I'm the Dragon Warrior. The fox and I are here on official Dragon Warrior business."

"Dragon who?" the first officer said.

"Warrior what?" the second officer added.

"Dragon Warrior," Po repeated. "Perhaps you know me better as *The Kung Fu Panda*." Po struck a hero pose.

Nope. They didn't. The officers threw them in a jail cart and laughed.

"Wait! Wait!" Po said. "I have a noodle restaurant named after me and everything!"

The officers walked off as the cart rolled over a bridge.

CHAPTER 13

"**O**kay, so we tried it your way," said Zhen. "Now we try mine." She removed her jade earring, connected it to her belt buckle, and the whole thing became a lock pick. Then, she used it to unlock the cart.

Zhen jumped out of the cart and off the bridge. She pulled Po along with her.

Fwoop! CRASH!

Zhen fell safely into a passing laundry cart. Po crashed into another cart being pulled by a goat. He accidentally destroyed the poor goat's cargo.

"Sorry!" Po said apologetically.

Zhen grabbed Po and they continued running.

"C'mon, c'mon, c'mon, c'mon!" Zhen chanted.

"You can't run away from the law. You're a wanted criminal," Po said to her.

"Yeah, well, it looks like I'm not the only one." Zhen pointed to a brand-new wanted sign of Zhen *and* Po.

Po was stunned. "Wow, city life really is fast-paced."

"We gotta get out of here before they call for . . ."

But before Zhen could finish her sentence, a herd of bull officers came rushing through.

". . . back-up."

"That is a lot of bull," Po said.

"Run!" Zhen cried.

Po and Zhen ran for their lives. While running, they grabbed bamboo poles from a nearby noodle shop. Zhen pole-vaulted over a wall. Po attempted to follow, but his pole broke, and he crashed through another noodle shop's wall.

The herd was right on their tails. "Let's go! Let's go!" Zhen called.

The duo ran into a busy market area. Then, they descended a sewer pipe, screaming as they traveled further downward.

It was all-out chaos! Po reached the end of the pipe first and, unfortunately, got stuck. Zhen then crashed into Po, which catapulted them onto a passing carriage. A group of bulls rounded a corner, running in their direction. Po directed the carriage down another alleyway, which sent the vehicle careening down a stairway. The cart bounced down the stairs as Po, Zhen, and the carriage drivers yelled, "Ah ah ah ah ah ah ah!"

At last, the carriage landed, flipping Po and then Zhen onto the nearby rooftops. They nearly slid off the roof, but Po managed to hang on with Zhen clinging on to his foot. They weren't safe for long.

A bull officer was still in pursuit. He grabbed at them. "I gotcha!" he said.

Po and Zhen, however, had another trick up their sleeves. They grabbed onto a nearby dragon kite and dashed around the city. Po wrangled the kite and aimed it directly downward. Zhen soon lost her balance, followed by Po. They tumbled toward the ground and grabbed onto other kite strings as they went. The kids holding the kite strings cheered, delighted by the adventure.

Po fell very slowly and landed on several strings of lights. He slid down rooftop after rooftop, finally landing in the street with Zhen. In a cruel twist of fate, Po crashed into the same goat merchant's cart, breaking it and smashing its cargo yet again.

"Sorry!" Po yelled out.

Po, Zhen, and the chasing bulls rushed into a nearby

shop where a bunny dusted her merchandise. The merchandise, of course, was delicate porcelain kitchenware.

The bunny gasped. Everyone tried to run delicately past the stacked tables of fine china. They narrowly slipped by. The bunny, relieved, sighed heavily and continued dusting her fragile and very breakable treasures.

Back on the streets, Po and Zhen made it into an alleyway filled with dozens of ornate kites, each one more lavish than the next. Zhen stopped in front of several drums.

"There they are," said a bull officer, heading directly toward them.

Zhen had a plan. She started drumming.

"Why are you drumming? We should be *running*!" Po grabbed frantically at Zhen, who was ignoring him. Did Zhen not see they were trapped?

But Zhen continued her drumming. The bulls closed in, getting nearer. Just then, a drum top swung open and revealed a secret door. Zhen hastily grabbed Po, stuffed him through the secret entrance, and climbed in behind him, closing the lid just in time. The bulls reached the drums and looked around, perplexed.

Po and Zhen had disappeared.

The secret door in the drum led down a drainage pipe. It was dim, dark, and damp, but at least there were no bulls chasing after them. Zhen led Po through the cramped maze of pipes.

"It isn't much farther now," Zhen assured Po.

"You always say that and it's always so much farther!"

The two emerged from the drainpipe and came to an underground den. Po saw that there were drainage pipes stretched in every direction, like tangled arteries—most were cracked and caked with green, spongy moss. Lanterns illuminated the space with a gloomy orange and green light.

"Whoa, what is this place?" Po asked.

"Home sweet home," replied Zhen.

It was the Den of Thieves, and it was filled with animal thieves, mercenaries, and cutthroats. It was a refuge for Juniper City's crooks and scoundrels. A boar nearby sharpened his tusks on a spinning turntable.

"Careful, these guys will steal your pants right off ya . . . you'll never even know it," Zhen warned Po.

Two monkeys named Teng and Tong popped out and smirked at each other. Po noticed three sweet-looking rabbit kids playing with a box of fireworks.

"Uh oh," said Po kindly. "Now, you kids be careful."

The bunnies growled and snapped their jaws onto his ears and nose.

"Ahhhh!" Po screamed.

Po turned and came face-to-face with the monkeys. They held Po's staff. "Huh?" Po said. "What? Alright. Give it back!"

He held out his hand and noticed the monkeys were now wearing his pants. The monkeys laughed. They were tricky! "Hey! Wait, you guys! Guys!"

The monkeys continued hopping around with Po's pants.

"Zhen!" Po pleaded.

Zhen gave the monkeys a double wedgie. Then she grabbed Po's pants and returned them and the Staff of Wisdom back to Po.

Po couldn't believe these were Zhen's friends.

"They're practically family," she said.

At that, there was a low, ominous voice rumbling from the pipes. "Zhen," it said, growing louder and closer until—suddenly—a boulder-sized ball came rolling out of the pipes and stopped before them.

The ball revealed itself to be a leather-faced pangolin named Han. He growled. The den inhabitants, each armed with a sharp weapon, circled Zhen and Po.

Po was terrified. Were they doomed?

Why had Zhen brought them *here*?

"Welcome home," Han said at last.

"Family, huh?" Po muttered to Zhen.

"More like distant cousins," she replied.

"So happy you've returned, Zhen. Now I can watch you die like I've always wanted."

"Han, old buddy," Zhen started. "Love what you did with the place! Is that new molding?" She pointed to the mold on the pipes.

Han wasn't in a laughing mood, though.

"You really don't want to do this," said Zhen.

"And why's that?"

"Because if you so much as lay one claw on me, you're going to have to answer to . . ." Zhen scrambled up on Po's shoulder. "*The Dragon Warrior!*"

Po puffed out his chest with pride. There was a brief moment of silence.

"Who?" said Han.

The surrounding thieves looked at one another; they were just as confused.

Po deflated. They'd never heard of him. "Are my adventures really that regional?"

"Introduce them, Po—" Zhen said as she climbed off Po and struck a fighting pose. "To. Your. Fists!"

Po cracked his knuckles, preparing to unleash a good, old-fashioned Dragon Warrior butt-kicking, when suddenly—

On Po's shoulders, two tiny versions of Master Shifu appeared with a **poof!** One was good and one was bad. "Remember, Po," said Good Master Shifu. "There are other ways to bring peace than by 'kicking butt.'"

"Yes. Now," said Bad Master Shifu impatiently.

"Wait. Hold on. Shouldn't my inner Shifus have differing opinions?"

Bad Master Shifu replied. "We are in total agreement—"

"—with our mutual disappointment—" added Good Master Shifu.

"—in you."

With that, the imaginary Master Shifus disappeared with another *poof!* Then, as the armed thieves were about to strike, Po cried out.

"Wait!"

The thieves stopped.

"He who resorts to violence now—" Po thought hard, mustering the most profound proverb he had in him, "—will only find more violence later."

Han and the rest of the thieves paused, thinking.

"So, what you're saying is—if we don't hurt Zhen a little now . . ." started an antelope.

"We can hurt her *a lot* later," a pig chimed in.

"What? No, that's not what I said." Po was dismayed.

"Yeah . . . and more violence *later* is better than less violence *now*," added Han.

"No, I—I think you're misunderstanding the fundamental point," Po said. The rabbit kids hopped up and down.

"More violence!" said one of the kids.

"Hooray!" shouted another.

"Violence makes my tummy tingle!" came the third.

Two of the rabbits listened to the other rabbit's tummy and giggled. Then, pleased by "more violence *later,*" all of the thieves dispersed.

"Wait! Come back!" Po called after them. "I'll come up with better wisdom!"

"You have got to workshop these proverbs," chided Zhen.

With the imminent threat gone—for now—they approached Han's meeting corner in the den. Po wanted Han to understand who he was.

"The son of Mr. Ping and Li?" Po said, hoping this would ring a bell.

"No," said Han.

"Mentored by Oogway?"

"No."

"Trained by Master Shifu?"

"Oh, Shifu! Yes!" Han replied.

"Ah-HA!" said Po with excitement.

"Everyone's heard of Shifu, the legendary magical squirrel," Han continued. "But not you." Then Han addressed Zhen. "Your black and white friend is interesting. I'm impressed he still has his pants. So, Zhen. What brings you crawling back to the den?"

"We just need some place to lie low for a while until the heat cools off," she answered.

"And why should we help you?"

"Because deep down, beneath that iron-scaled exterior, is a good-hearted soul who actually cares about the well-being of his fellow scoundrels," said Zhen.

The rabbits brought over a tray of tea to Po.

"Thank you," Po said to them. He lifted the cup to his lips, but Zhen slapped it out of his paw.

"Don't drink that," she warned.

The spilled tea sizzled through the ground as the rabbit children skipped away, giggling.

"Fine," said Han, continuing their conversation. "But if you're still here by nightfall, I'm calling the bulls myself."

Zhen held out her paw for Han to shake. "You won't regret this."

"But you will," replied Han ominously.

Zhen stared at him.

"Ahh sorry," he laughed. "I meant to say that in my head. Sleep tight." Han curled into a ball and rolled away, back into the pipes.

Po took a deep breath. All they had to do now was take down The Chameleon—once and for all.

Well, *almost* all they had to do.

First, they had to get Po's pants back.

Again.

Those monkeys sure were fast!

CHAPTER 14

Li and Mr. Ping came upon the dockside tavern.

"This place doesn't look very friendly," said Li warily.
Inside, the tavern patrons were nursing their kung fu–inflicted wounds, looking a little worse for wear. "Ooh, my tail," one of them groaned.

Mr. Ping cringed. "I'm sure everything is fine." He jumped down from the stack of dishes he was standing on. "This is a restaurant. These are my people. We speak the same language. You wait here!"

Inside the tavern, Granny Boar was back to playing mahjong with her patrons. She was rather taken aback when she heard a bright and peppy greeting—

"Salutations!" Mr. Ping grinned eagerly. "Hi, everybody. I'm so sorry to interrupt, ahaha. I know you're having a good time, but I was wondering if a panda happened to be passing by here?"

Granny Boar stared him down.

"There *was* a panda here," she growled slowly. "You know him?" She stood up on the table, a group of angry boars flanking her from behind.

"Know him?" Mr. Ping replied obliviously. "Why, I'm his dad!"

Several of the bar patrons grabbed Mr. Ping by the neck. He struggled to get free, crying, "Quack! Quack! Quack!"

"You need to pay for what your son did to my tavern," Granny Boar hissed.

Mr. Ping surveyed the crumbling tavern and spotted a Po-shaped hole in a nearby wall. Oops.

"My boy wouldn't have done this for no reason," Mr. Ping croaked. "Is it possible your broth was bland?"

"Try it!" said Granny Boar. She pulled his head over a piping hot bowl of soup—hot enough it could scorch an unsuspecting goose.

"Whoa! No! Nooo! The broth smells excellent!" Mr. Ping assured her.

Granny Boar let out a menacing cackle.

"You should not add a single thing!" Mr. Ping begged her. "Especially not *meee*!"

Granny Boar was about to dunk Mr. Ping's head into the steaming bowl of soup when—

"*Let him go.*"

Mr. Ping and Granny Boar looked over at the tavern entrance, where there was a panda-shaped silhouette backlit in the doorway.

The patrons gasped.

The bunny server ducked under the bar to hide.

"The panda's back!"

"He's back!"

Li slowly entered the tavern. "No, but you're about to wish he was. 'Cause if you think *he* made a mess of this place, you have no idea what I'm capable of. Everything he learned, he learned from *me*."

The tavern patrons stared, frightened by Li's threats.

"Except one thing," Li continued. "*Mercy.* I don't know where he got that because I don't believe in it."

Li looked formidable, and Mr. Ping chuckled slyly under his breath.

"Now, this can go one of two ways. The easy way, in which you tell me where he is. Or the hard way, in which you tell me where he is, but it's hard to understand what you're saying because you have no teeth." Li was trying his best to look fierce. Mr. Ping thought it was working wonderfully.

Granny Boar looked unsettled. Li grabbed a cup from a nearby bunny waiter's tray, downed the drink, and crushed the cup. Not the best idea—some of the cup's shards lodged into Li's paw. The tavern-goers gasped as Li winced in pain. Then, Li approached a table, grabbed a bunch of mahjong tiles, and put them in his mouth.

"Mahjong?" he said, the noise garbled through the tiles. "I eat mahjong tiles for breakfast!" **_CRUNCH!_** He spat out a tooth on the table. Li turned away, hiding the fact that he was clutching his cheek in pain.

"Oooh," he continued, trying to be menacing.

Li jumped on a table, grabbed some chopsticks, and broke them in half; he was doing his best to imitate one of Po's kung fu poses. Then Li got up on one leg in the crane pose. As he did so, the table snapped from underneath him, but Li maintained the pose on the broken surface.

Outside, the tavern building, which was already off-kilter from the tussle with Po and Zhen, teetered precariously under Li's weight.

Inside, the patrons waited anxiously. A wolf dropped Mr. Ping, who let out a "Quack!" The patrons sprinted to one side of the tavern, attempting to realign the building.

The structure righted itself again, balanced safely on its perch . . . at least for the moment.

Li smiled. He could make the whole building collapse if he wanted to!

Li trapped Granny Boar and the other tavern patrons in a corner.

"Where's our son?" Li demanded.

"He took a boat to Juniper City!" Granny replied.

"Which way?" said Mr. Ping.

The crowd all pointed in the same direction.

"You know a wise goose once—" Li started to say.

Mr. Ping grabbed his arm. "Time to go!"

Outside, Li and Mr. Ping closed the tavern door behind them. They breathed heavily. They were shocked that they got away with Li's "tough panda" ruse, but it had worked. Don't mess with dads on a mission! And best yet, they knew where Po was!

From inside the tavern, several of the bunny waiters came hopping out of the window and landed next to Li and Mr. Ping. With their sudden movement, the tavern shifted more off-kilter, and—*SPLASH!*—plummeted off the cliffside and into the water.

The tavern patrons and Granny Boar crawled out of the chimney and stood atop the roof of the floating tavern. They were alive, but their battle against Mr. Ping and Li had ended in defeat.

The bunnies, however, cheered. They had long been the tavern's disrespected and underappreciated waitstaff. Thanks to Mr. Ping and Li, they were now free from the patronizing patrons and Granny Boar's wrath—forever.

"I *hate* pandas," Granny Boar grumbled.

CHAPTER 15

At dusk, Zhen and Po climbed up the roof of a tower in The Chameleon's fortress.

"I know I promised that I'd lead you right to The Chameleon's *front door*, but—" Zhen whispered to Po, "the back door seems a little more practical."

"I gotta say, Zhen, you really are a fox of your word." Po held out a peach pit to Zhen.

"What is this?" Zhen asked.

"Consider it a little token of my appreciation."

"A chewed-up peach pit?"

Po smiled. It wasn't just *any* chewed-up peach pit. It was from Master Oogway's Peach Tree of Heavenly Wisdom!

"It's a Valley of Peace thing," Po explained. "I carry it

around to remind me that every pit holds the strength of a mighty tree. Maybe it'll do the same for you."

Zhen took the peach pit and studied it. She didn't want to admit it, but she couldn't remember the last time someone *gave* her something. Usually, she'd have to steal it. Even if it was a chewed-up peach pit. The gesture was nice, albeit a bit gross.

"Hey, Po?" Zhen asked. "Are you sure you wanna do this?"

"Yes. For how may one kick butt, if one doesn't seek a butt to kick?" Po said wisely.

Zhen climbed into the sewer tunnel. "You're a real piece of work, you know that?"

"Thank you," said Po, heartened. "Wait, wait, wait. Was that a compliment or an insult?"

"Little of this, little of that," she replied.

Mr. Ping and Li arrived in Juniper City. Like Po before them, they, too, were overwhelmed. Forget noodle shops and dumplings—they had never before seen so much hustle and bustle!

Mr. Ping held up a picture of Po to a bunny.

"Have you seen our son?" he asked.

The bunny shook his head.

They stopped and asked a boar.

"Sorry," the boar replied.

Then an antelope.

No dice.

A croc.

"No," said the croc.

And a bull.

The bull had not.

A sheep?

"Naaaahhh," the sheep replied.

Just when they thought they were out of luck, Li found a piece of fur on the ground. He picked it up.

"YES!" Li said confidently to Mr. Ping. "Po was here. We pandas have a gift for seeing what others cannot. Come on. There may be more clues up ahead."

Li pulled Mr. Ping forward as they came upon hundreds of wanted posters, each one emblazoned with Po's smiling face staring back at them.

Po poked his head through an opening in the fortress and came face-to-face with a sleeping Komodo dragon guard.

"Ahh—" Zhen quickly covered Po's mouth and shushed him. They were in "do or die" mode.

Po and Zhen emerged from the manhole and found the entrance to The Chameleon's vault room guarded by Komodo dragons. Well, "guarded" was perhaps giving them too much credit. They were all snoring.

"Shhh," said Zhen.

She slowly maneuvered around the Komodo dragon guards. Po set down the manhole cover gingerly, but his movement wasn't ginger enough, and it rolled toward the staircase . . . *loudly*. The lid barreled down the seemingly infinite steps. Zhen pinched her nose in annoyance. A Komodo dragon guard rolled over onto his back, still asleep.

Phew!

Po and Zhen safely passed the guards. The duo celebrated with a silent high five. Zhen's tail accidentally brushed Po's nose, however, and he geared up to sneeze. Quickly, Zhen plugged his nose, which—hooray!—worked. But all the trapped air inside the big panda became too much, and it released a teeny, tiny fart.

PFFFFT!

The sound (or was it the smell? Zhen wasn't sure) awoke the Komodo dragon guards. They pointed their weapons in Po and Zhen's direction and growled.

Then began the chase.

Po and Zhen ran through the vault room door. Without thinking, Po pressed down on two nearby levers. The doors shut and trapped the guards outside, but at the same time, a booby trap activated. Po and Zhen gasped.

The metal layers of the door released sharp, spinning shapes that they had to dodge. They jumped and ducked, evading each set skillfully. As the last of the spinners sprung forth, Po somersaulted down the stairs of the vault room with Zhen following behind.

"Whoa, that was close," Po said. But as he stepped forward, another trap was triggered.

"Look out!" Zhen called.

"Huh?"

WHAM!

A massive cage crashed down from the ceiling. It slammed down and encased Po.

Zhen jumped to her feet and rushed toward him. "Are you okay?"

"Stand back," Po instructed her.

Po unleashed a powerful kung fu fist into the bars of the cage.

BAM! A glyph on the cage glowed, but the bars refused to bend.

"EVEN THE WORST OF US CAN BRING OUT THE BEST."

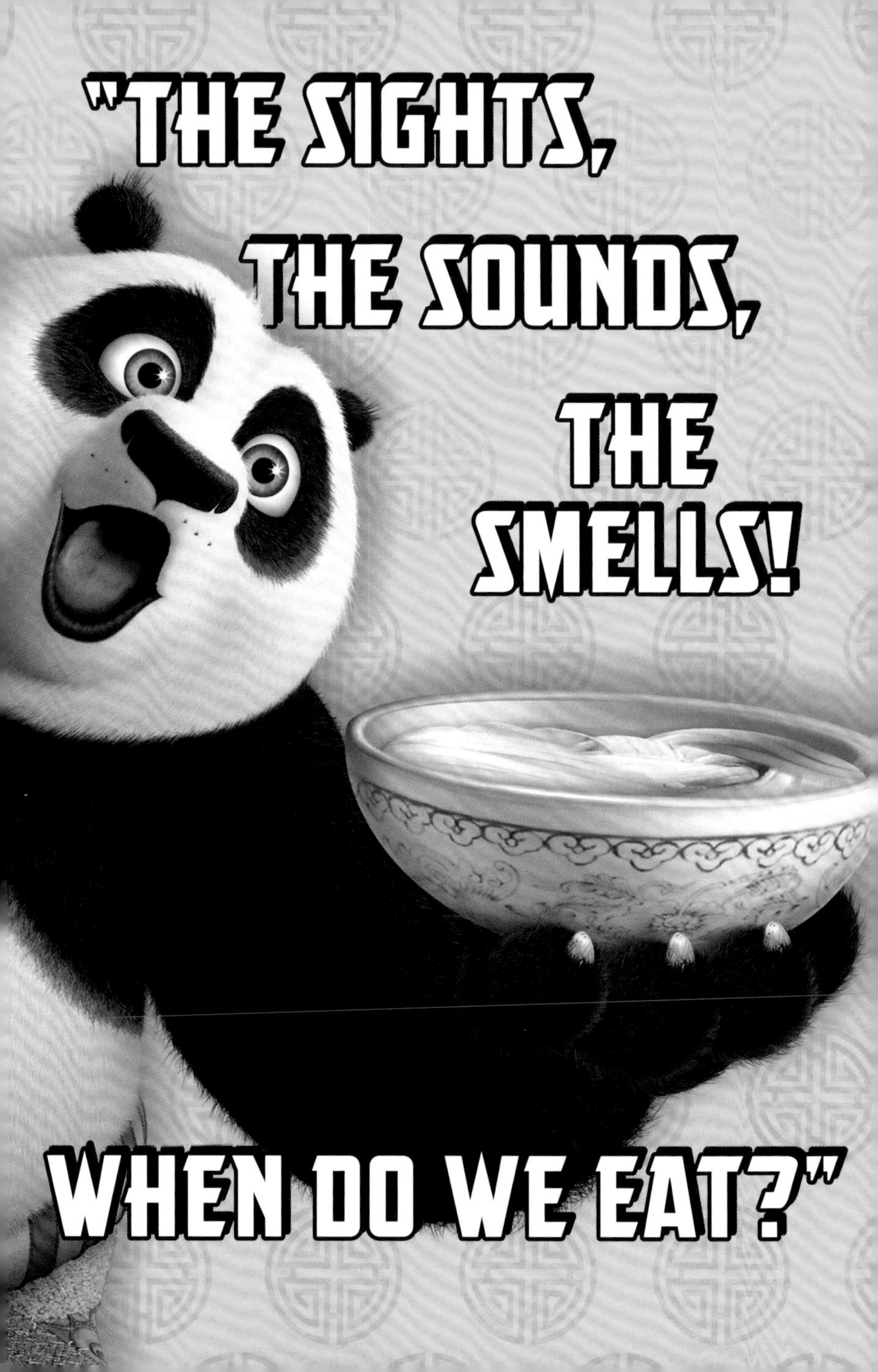
"THE SIGHTS,
THE SOUNDS,
THE SMELLS!
WHEN DO WE EAT?"

A cage that kept the Dragon Warrior inside?

"The bars must be made of some kind of magic . . ."

But there was no time for speculation. Zhen heard someone coming. With Po still inside, Zhen desperately tried to lift the cage, but it was no use. The cage was too heavy for a small fox.

Po had a new idea.

"You brace it. I'll lift," he said to Zhen. "Take this." He thrust the Staff of Wisdom through the bars and at Zhen.

Zhen hesitated. Then she grasped onto the Staff of Wisdom with her paw.

"Alright, stand back. Here I go." Po attempted to lift the cage off himself. But he noticed that Zhen wasn't helping at all. "Zhen?"

Po looked outside of the cage. There Zhen was. And there was Po's staff.

And there was Zhen, backing away.

"Where are you taking my staff?" he asked her.

"I think you mean *my* staff," came a menacing voice. It was The Chameleon! Zhen slowly and somberly handed the Staff of Wisdom to The Chameleon.

The Chameleon faced Po. "You gave it to Zhen, and now Zhen has given it to me. The staff must be given in order to gain its power."

Wait . . . what? Po thought. *All this time . . . Zhen had been helping The Chameleon?* Po felt hurt and betrayed.

"Zhen," Po pleaded with her.

"First rule of the streets," Zhen said calmly, although she was shaking. "Never trust anyone."

"*Ha!*" cackled The Chameleon. "Don't tell me you actually thought my young apprentice was your friend?"

"Apprentice?" Po looked at Zhen incredulously. Then it sunk in. "The Chameleon is the one that took you in?"

The Chameleon smiled. "Best thing that ever happened to her. You should've seen the little gutter snipe before I found her. Mangy and half-starved. Hanging out with those criminal rejects from the Den of Thieves. But I took her under my wing. Taught her how to be strong, ruthless, cunning. I made her what she is today."

"So, you went through all of this just to get me to give you the Staff of Wisdom?" Po asked. "Why?"

"I rose to power because I can take any form I desire," The Chameleon said. To demonstrate this, she transformed into different forms—a rhino, a wolf, a gorilla, a crocodile. "Unfortunately, form is not the same as function."

Po blinked. "I don't think that answers my question," he replied.

The Chameleon transformed herself into Tai Lung.

"Just because I can *look* like Tai Lung doesn't mean I can *fight* like him. All looks, no skill." She transformed back into her chameleon self. "I'm afraid it's true what they say about me. I *am* a fraud. But thanks to the Staff of Wisdom, all that's going to change. You see, Po, it's the spirit that houses the body's knowledge, and now that I have access to the Spirit Realm . . . all that knowledge will soon be mine. Once I possess all the skills of every opponent that ever faced the Dragon Warrior, no one will ever dare question my power again."

"You forgot about me," Po said, slamming his fists against the bars of the cage. But it still was no use—the bars didn't budge.

"Oh, don't bother, Po. Those bars are enchanted with some very old and very powerful magic. You'd need ten Dragon Warriors to get through them."

"Then I won't go through them," Po said, determinedly. "*I'll go under them.*"

Po directed his fist at the stone floor beneath his feet and punched.

"Yahhhhhhh!" he screamed.

His battle cry was powerful as he struck his move. Below them was another floor filled with Komodo dragon guards.

On Po's move, the floor's baroque ceiling burst open

with a **SMASH!**, and Po fell in the center of the room, surrounded by rubble and plaster debris.

"Wahh!" Po yelped as he fell.

"Wha—?" said one of the guards.

"Guards!" The Chameleon screeched from above.

The guards launched at Po.

Po staggered backward and tripped, causing a huge cloud of dust to billow up around them.

A fist connected with Po's face and Po's foot kicked a henchman back. **Wham, wham, wham!** Po's fist punched another, and another! Po met each guard's attempt to attack with a fierce move.

A group of the guards descended on Po. With a singular punch, he managed to get them all off him. Po may not have the Staff of Wisdom, but he was still the Dragon Warrior.

Po stumbled out of the dust cloud just as a Komodo dragon guard followed, its claws outstretched. Po grabbed the guard's tail and swung him around. Po spun again, spotted a door, and ran toward it. The henchmen hurled their spears.

A shrill whistle wailed; it was the unmistakable whistle of approaching spears behind Po. Po twisted himself into an impressive shape to avoid all the attacking spears.

Then, the door swung open.

The door led to a parapet—a low, protective wall at the edge of The Chameleon's fortress—that opened to the night sky. Po flopped off the swinging door in time to see the guards charging toward it. He slammed the door shut and jammed a spear through its handles, which blocked the door from re-opening and the Komodo dragon guards from coming out. Just as he was about to dust himself off, Po turned to see two guards standing watch. They brandished their weapons and charged.

"Ah!" Po turned and ran back toward the door, but instead of going through, he ran straight up and flipped backward. It was an awesome move!

WHAM!

The guards' spears missed Po and pierced the door instead. Po landed behind the guards, who were now unarmed, and grabbed them both by their belts. He flung them toward the balcony railing and they slid off the edge. "Whaaaaaa!" they screamed as they fell toward their doom.

"Po!" a familiar voice called.

"Zhen?"

Zhen ran toward Po. Interestingly, she was carrying the Staff of Wisdom.

"My staff! Hand it over," Po demanded.

"I'm so sorry I lied to you," Zhen said.

"We'll talk about it later," said Po. "Right now, we have to stop The Chameleon."

"Po!" boomed another voice. Another . . . *familiar* voice.

Po turned around, confused, to see yet *another* Zhen running toward him.

"Zhen?" Po asked, mouth agape.

Po looked down to see the scaly, reptilian hand of The Chameleon, disguised as Zhen, on his arm.

But it was too late. The Chameleon (still disguised as Zhen) swung the Staff of Wisdom into Po.

"Whoa!" Po screamed. "Aahhhhh!"

The Chameleon was too powerful. Po fell backward, off the parapet, and into the unknown.

The two Zhens watched as Po's panda body descended into the misty chasm below. There was no surviving that fall. It was surely the end of the Dragon Warrior.

The Chameleon transformed back into herself.

"Do you have a problem, Zhen?" she asked.

"You never said you were gonna hurt him."

"I didn't hurt him. I *killed* him," The Chameleon replied, remorseless. "You know, Zhen, when I lifted you out of the gutter and into the glamor, it's because I saw a bit of myself in you. Now, I don't quite know what I see. But whatever it is, I don't like it."

"I'm sorry," said Zhen. She cast her gaze into the misty chasm. "Really, really sorry."

The Chameleon snapped her fingers. "Good girl. Chop, chop! We have a Spirit Realm to plunder. And smile. Nobody likes a grouch. Honestly, Zhen, I don't know where you pick up such bad habits."

CHAPTER 16

Deep, deep, deep down in the misty abyss, Po desperately clung onto a branch.

"Alright," said Po, struggling.

Nearby, a Komodo dragon guard skittered up the cliff. He spotted Po. The guard growled.

"Hey there," Po said nervously.

The guard lunged at Po and grabbed hold of him.

"Ah! Whoa!"

Po lost his grip on the branch. He slid down but managed to regain his grip on the cliffside. The Komodo dragon guard would not let go. He was still clutching the panda tightly.

"Aha! Get off me! Ow! Ow! Ahhh!" Po shook back and forth, attempting to dislodge the guard.

"Son!" a familiar voice shouted.

Po looked up and saw Mr. Ping, coming to Po's rescue.

"Ahhhh!" Mr. Ping screeched.

"Dad!"

Mr. Ping kicked the Komodo dragon guard off Po. But the resulting force caused Mr. Ping to fly back in midair.

"Now save me! Ahh!" cried Mr. Ping.

Po grabbed him.

"Dad," Po said again.

"Hi, son," said Mr. Ping.

Po was about to slip again when another panda paw snatched his wrist. And not just any panda paw. It was Li's! Li was expertly hanging off a branch.

"*Dads*!" Po said. He could hardly believe it.

Li strenuously reeled Po and Mr. Ping up onto his branch. Together, the trio made it up to a demolished portion of The Chameleon's fortress. Then Li gently placed Po and Mr. Ping down, no longer in danger of the fall.

"Oh, Po, are you alright?" asked Li.

Mr. Ping examined their son. "Are you hurt? How do you feel?"

But Po was still shocked. "What are you two doing here?"

Mr. Ping blinked at him. "We were worried."

"*He* was worried," Li clarified.

"Don't give me that," said Mr. Ping to Li. "You were worried, too."

"Fine, I was worried, too," Li admitted.

"So you followed me?" Po asked.

"It was *his* idea," Li pointed at Mr. Ping, who grunted. "Okay, okay. It was both our ideas."

"We only follow because we love," said Mr. Ping.

But Po didn't think that was it.

"You followed because after all I've done, you still don't think I'm capable of taking care of myself," he muttered.

"And because we love?" said Mr. Ping hopefully.

Po slumped, feeling defeated.

"Well, you're right," he said. "I messed up. I trusted the wrong person, I walked into a trap, and to top it all off, I gave the Staff of Wisdom right to The Chameleon."

"Oh, Po." Mr. Ping put a wing on Po's shoulder.

"If only I'd listened to Master Shifu and stayed in the Valley of Peace. I wound up making everything worse. I was just so determined to keep things the way they are."

"Everyone is afraid of change, Po. Even me. There was a time—not so long ago—when all I wanted to be was the greatest noodle chef in the valley," said Mr. Ping.

"So what happened?" asked Po.

"I became the greatest noodle chef in the valley!"

"He knows how to cook a good noodle," Li shrugged.

"But I also became a father," Mr. Ping continued. "And nothing, *nothing's* ever been the same since. Change doesn't always have to be a bad thing. Why do you think I always change the menu at the restaurant?"

Po didn't know.

"Because if things stayed the same forever, sooner or later, they would lose their flavor."

Po thought about that for a moment.

"It's true, Po," added Li. "I mean, just look at me. Before I left my village, I was timid. Nervous. Afraid of my own shadow. But now—"

CRACK!

"Ah!" yelped Li. He jumped into Mr. Ping's arms. Mr. Ping collapsed under his weight.

"Move it! This way!" a Komodo dragon guard shouted and cracked a whip.

Still in their hideout and undetected by the guards, Po watched as hundreds of cages were carted up to The Chameleon's fortress.

"This looks bad," remarked Li.

"Move it!" the guards continued to shout.

"*Really, really bad,*" Po agreed.

"Tonight, when the Blood Moon rises to its highest point in the night sky, I will open the door to the Spirit Realm and all of its secrets will be mine!" The Chameleon declared. She gazed upward. The Blood Moon was still very low, and barely any light filtered through the oculus in the ceiling.

"Ugh, does the Blood Moon always rise this slowly?" She pondered this impatiently. "I seem to remember it rising faster . . . No? Just me?"

The Komodo dragon guards surrounding The Chameleon shrugged.

Still fixated on the moon, The Chameleon waited. And waited . . . and waited. Finally, she was bored of waiting.

"It's just for dramatic effect anyway. I think I'm just going to open the Spirit Realm now."

With that, The Chameleon spun the Staff of Wisdom. Embers burst forth in a show of light and color. Illuminated glyphs and smoke met to form a glowing portal—a portal to the Spirit Realm.

"Bring me Tai Lung," The Chameleon said.

From deep within the portal came a familiar growl. Zhen shielded herself from the bright light.

A silhouette appeared in the Spirit Realm. It emerged

from the vortex and enveloped the room in a mystical plume of smoke. Within the ethereal glow stood the *real* Tai Lung. The Chameleon had accomplished her goal.

"Tai Lung. *Big fan*," said The Chameleon, introducing herself to him.

Tai Lung took in the scene.

"What is this? Who are you and what are you doing with that staff?"

"This staff was recently given to me by an old friend of yours," The Chameleon replied.

"That false Dragon Warrior?" Tai Lung scoffed. "Po might be an idiot, but he'd never willingly hand over Oogway's staff to the likes of you."

The Chameleon smiled coyly. "Whoever said anything about him handing it over willingly?"

The vault room opened to reveal dozens of magical cages, all waiting to be filled with master villains from the Spirit Realm. Zhen looked on, ashamed of her role in The Chameleon's plan.

Tai Lung grinned, impressed. "Mmm. Apparently, I misjudged you, lizard. Now, why have you summoned me back to the Mortal Realm?"

"I summoned you here so that you could teach me your most legendary kung fu moves."

"Then you've gone to a lot of trouble for nothing. I'd sooner die again than divulge my secrets to you."

"It wasn't a request," The Chameleon said simply.

With that, a squadron of Komodo dragon guards surrounded Tai Lung. The guards charged at him but were clearly no match for the powerful fighter. Using his martial arts prowess, Tai Lung easily dispatched them and kicked one straight past The Chameleon.

The Chameleon shapeshifted into an imposing elephant.

Tai Lung roared at the elephant, and they began their fight. The Chameleon dodged Tai Lung's attacks, changing into a bear, then a wolf. At one point, she blocked Tai Lung with the Staff of Wisdom.

Tai Lung continued his onslaught. The Chameleon evaded him, jumped to a higher level, and turned back into her original form. Tai Lung kicked into the ground, unleashing a wave of energy through the room.

The Chameleon flung her tongue out at Tai Lung. He grabbed it, swung her around, and then used his signature move—The Nerve Strike—to pummel The Chameleon to the ground. **POW!**

Tai Lung grabbed her. "Your magic tricks are impressive, but they're no match for years of kung fu training." He had been Master Shifu's student before Po, after all.

The Chameleon grinned devilishly. "Unfortunately, I don't have that kind of time to wait."

Her long tongue shot out and slithered into Tai Lung's ear. Then, in one fell move, she absorbed Tai Lung's powers. Zhen watched in horror as Tai Lung's skills were leeched from his body.

The Chameleon transformed into Tai Lung.

"Hee yah!" The Chameleon yelled in Tai Lung's form. "At last, I'm finally complete!"

The Chameleon unleashed Tai Lung's own Nerve Attack back at him, sending him flying into a cage.

"Impossible," muttered the real Tai Lung.

"Form *and* function," said The Chameleon.

A cage door swung shut on the real Tai Lung, imprisoning him. Their brawl was over. The Chameleon walked away and morphed back into her chameleon form.

"And that's just the beginning," she said.

The Chameleon laughed as she picked up the Staff of Wisdom from the ground and reopened the portal to the Spirit Realm.

Zhen crouched down in guilt-ridden silence. She had Po's peach pit and studied it pensively, flipping it through her fingers. *Peach pit.* What had Po said about the peach pit again?

"I carry it around to remind me that every pit holds the strength of a mighty tree."

After a moment, Zhen got up and ran determinedly out of The Chameleon's vault room.

CHAPTER 17

Outside, where the Komodo dragon guards were hauling up cages, Mr. Ping grabbed hold of Po's leg.

"Po, wait! Please, be reasonable!" he hollered.

"I'm not going anywhere until I get my staff back," Po said determinedly.

"No staff is worth your life," Li said.

"It's not my life I'm worried about," Po replied.

Mr. Ping let go of Po's leg.

Po continued. "It's true. I might not be the Dragon Warrior forever, but while I still am, I won't let anyone else get hurt because of me."

Po walked away. Mr. Ping and Li watched their beloved son leave.

"He makes me proud," said Mr. Ping. "But also, angry."

"Ah, the joys of parenthood," Li agreed.

Zhen descended the steps of the fortress.

She moved as fast as she could. When she saw Po approach, his panda self clearly alive and well, she had to blink twice to be sure it was really him.

"Po! You're alive!"

"Yeah, no thanks to you," he said. He pushed past her and moved on up the steps.

"Please, I made a mistake," Zhen begged.

"So did I. *Trusting you.*"

Zhen moved in front of Po. "I'm sorry."

"Yeah, I bet. Did your master tell you to say that, too?"

"She's not my master," said Zhen defensively. "I'm leaving. For good."

"Why should I believe you?"

"Because it's the truth."

Po continued to walk up the stairs. Zhen tried to push him backward.

"What are you doing?"

"Stopping you," Zhen said.

"Get out of my way, Zhen."

"*No,*" she insisted.

"For the last time . . . move." Po gritted his teeth.

"You want me to move?" Zhen asked. "Move me."

"First, you betray me, and now you want to fight me?"
Zhen swiped at Po. It was on.

Po and Zhen exchanged a flurry of kicks and blows.
Although Po was clearly more skilled, Zhen's agility and
trickery managed to keep her a step ahead at every turn.
The pair fought on.

"Why are you doing this?" Po said to her.

Mr. Ping and Li appeared behind them and watched
with concern as the two battled.

"To stop you from getting killed!" Zhen cried.

More punches were thrown. Zhen and Po sailed through
the air as they kicked at each other.

"Why do you care if I get killed or not?" Po asked. He
again walked past Zhen.

Zhen balled up her fists and turned to rush at Po in one
last act of desperation—but instead of an attack, she held
her arms wide for an embrace.

"Because you're my friend," Zhen said. "The only real
friend I've ever had."

Po was touched at first, but then he remembered that

Zhen had tricked him before. He hardened his glance and stepped away from her hug.

"First rule of the streets: *never trust anyone*. Right, Zhen? You taught me well."

"Po!" Zhen fell to the ground and watched him go. She realized that he was right, that everything transpiring now was a consequence of her actions.

Mr. Ping and Li ran up behind Zhen.

"We should never have let him come here. We are such terrible fathers," Mr. Ping said to Li.

"I'm a terrible friend," breathed Zhen. She was talking to herself, but Mr. Ping answered anyway.

"Well, that's true. You're worse."

"There has to be something we can do," said Li.

"What can we do? There's just three of us against an army," Mr. Ping lamented.

Three of us? That gave Zhen an idea. "Then I guess we'll just have to get an army of our own," she said.

Mr. Ping and Li exchanged a confused look.

Down in the Den of Thieves, it was business as usual. The rabbits were playing with a single looted stiletto, and the monkeys had a box of stolen goods. Thievery and trickery and looting ran amok. That is, until Zhen rushed into the den. Mr. Ping and Li followed closely behind her.

"Hey! Listen up, everybody!" yelled Zhen.

Nobody listened. Zhen jumped on a barrel, trying to grab everyone's attention. It didn't work.

"QUAAACK!"

Li held Mr. Ping in the air, amplifying his quack. At this, the crowd quieted down. "The Dragon Warrior's in trouble!" she announced.

No reaction.

"Who?" said one of the thieves.

"You know. Po," replied Zhen.

Silence.

"*The panda*," Zhen tried again.

The monkeys looked at Li.

"A different panda."

"I'm his father," offered Li.

"I'm *also* his father," added Mr. Ping. "What matters is that my friend is in trouble, and he needs my help," Zhen continued. "So, I need yours!"

"And why should we help you?" boomed a voice. It was Han, the pangolin.

Zhen hesitated. "Because . . ." Then she remembered

Po's earlier words. She needed to channel him and his can-do attitude. "It's the right thing to do."

The thieves stared at Zhen for a moment. Then they laughed loudly.

"Look, I know you think it might be too late for a bunch of cheats, thieves, and cutthroats like us to change our ways. But a good friend once told me: it's never too late to do the right thing," Zhen continued, unrelenting.

The group considered her words.

"So," Han chimed in, "what you're saying is, the more 'right' we do now . . . the more 'wrong' we can do later?"

"What?" Zhen said. "No, that's—"

"And with The Chameleon out of the way . . ." the antelope mused.

". . . we can finally do all the 'wrong' we want!" finished the pig.

"I think you're missing the fundamental point—" Zhen was cut off once again.

"*The streets will run red with the blood of our enemies,*" one of the rabbits whispered.

The crooks all grew eager with ominous approval.

"Okay, whatever," said Zhen, giving up. "Are you ready to do the right thing for the wrong reason?"

Bloodthirsty cheers rang throughout the den.

"Violence! Violence! Violence! Violence! Violence! Violence!" the thieves chanted.

It was better than nothing. Zhen would just have to make it work.

❖ III ❖

CHAPTER 18

A quartet of Komodo dragon guards patrolled The Chameleon's fortress, chatting as they made their watchful rounds.

"Now, you see, the mistake this Dragon Warrior fella made was underestimating his opponent. I never would have walked into such an obvious trap," said one of the guards as if he knew everything.

A voice interrupted them.

"Hey," it said.

The Komodo dragon guards turned around and gasped. The voice belonged to Po! And Po was ready to kick some Komodo dragon butt.

Within moments, the four guards were tied together by their tails.

"Now, you see, the mistake this Dragon Warrior fella made here was—" the boastful guard started to say in an attempt to regain some dignity, but he was abruptly cut off.

"Quit talking, Larry," grumbled another guard.

Po smiled. He wasn't making any mistakes now. He made his way through the gloomy hallways of the fortress and approached the vault room. Then, Po snuck in.

Little did Po know, from another part of the fortress, Zhen, Li, and Mr. Ping were cooking up a plan.

"This place is crawling with more guards than I've ever seen," Zhen whispered to Mr. Ping and Li. "I'm never gonna get to Po in time."

Li looked up the wall. He smiled. He'd just come up with a plan.

"You just get to Po. We'll take care of the guards," he told her.

That was news to Mr. Ping.

"We will, huh?" Mr. Ping said. Then, he puffed his chest, remembering who he was protecting. "I—I mean, *we will.*" Then, to Li, he asked quietly, "But how?"

Li brimmed with confidence. "Just leave that to me."

The Chameleon continued summoning great villain spirits out of the Spirit Realm. Then, like she had done with Tai Lung, she used her tongue to strip them of their kung fu skills and claim their prowess as her own.

A rhino. A pig. A crocodile. A bear. The Chameleon stole each of their moves and then tossed them carelessly into magical cages.

From his hiding spot, Po's eyes widened as he watched a wolf spirit meet the same fate. By this point, hundreds of broken spirits sat trapped in The Chameleon's enchanted cages. They may have been villains once, but now they looked weak, gray, and hollow.

"What's going on here?" Po whispered.

"The Chameleon is pulling us from the Spirit Realm and draining us of all our powers," a bear replied.

"And she's using Oogway's staff to do it," a rhino said.

Po furrowed his brow. "I'm here to get it back," he said.

"Huh," said the fire-breathing crocodile. "I won't hold my breath."

"Um, I'm sorry, do I know you?" Po asked.

"Do you know me?" the croc replied, clearly insulted. "It's Scott. *The fire-breathing crocodile*." Scott showed off a little of his fire breathing to prove his point.

"Oh, right! Scott!" Po said. *Scott, not Steve*. "Master

Shifu and I were just talking about you."

Before Scott could reply, a voice interrupted.

"Panda," the voice said. "Oogway made a mistake choosing you as the Dragon Warrior."

Po turned to see yellow eyes glowing from a cage nearby. It was Tai Lung.

"I just didn't realize how big a mistake it was until now," Tai Lung continued. "First, you send me to the Spirit Realm. Then, I'm dragged back here by the staff that you gave away."

"I'll get the staff back, restore your powers, and return you all to the Spirit Realm. You'll see," Po said, determined.

* ❀ 囍 ❀ *

Meanwhile, Mr. Ping and Li were ready to enact Li's plan.

An intimidating squadron of Komodo dragon guards passed by. Li puffed out his chest. He was channeling his "tough bear" act from the tavern.

"Alright, you bunch of cantankerous Komodos," he threatened. "Now, this can go one of two ways. The easy way, in which you surrender willingly. Or the hard way, where you surrender woundedly. Haha, the choice is yours."

The guards stared quizzically at each other.

A moment later, Li ran horrified from the fortress as the Komodo dragon guards chased him away.

"I was kidding! I was kidding!" Li called back to them. The crowd of guards chasing him seemed to be growing larger and larger. "Ahhhhhh!"

But Li's plan wasn't finished. This, too, was a ruse! The guards didn't know it yet, but Li had led them right into a trap. He smiled next to Mr. Ping, who was lounging in a nearby lawn chair. Li sat down next to him and took a drink from Mr. Ping.

The guards watched, baffled.

Then they heard the unmistakable sound of . . . creepy rabbit giggling?

Three adorable rabbits emerged; their eyes were as big as saucers and they had fluffy tails.

"Awww," said one of the guards.

The rabbits' faces turned from cute to deadly.

"Huh?" said another guard.

The rabbits pounced. As it just so happened, they, too, were part of the trap. Thieves, tricksters, and scoundrels of all sorts sprang into attack against the guards.

"Ah, ah, ah!" screeched one Komodo dragon guard as a bunny chomped on his shoulder.

"Run away!" screamed another guard.

Han the pangolin stood above the chaos. "Cannonball!" he yelled as he ricocheted off the ledge. He crashed into the Komodo dragon squadron like a bowling ball and took down the guards as if they were pins.

The horde of thieves then took out The Chameleon's guards one by one. The rabbits were working together as an impressive acrobatic team, smashing through many of the Komodo dragons.

From their lawn chairs, Mr. Ping eyed Li's drink. He wanted to know what Li thought about it.

"Oh? Is it too spicy?" asked Mr. Ping.

"No. It's got just the perfect *kick*," replied Li. He watched a monkey thief kick a guard.

"Ginseng," said Mr. Ping. "That's the secret to my mulberry punch."

"That panda was right!" yelled one of the rabbits.

"More violence later *is* better!"

Their menacingly sweet giggles filled the air.

As the fighting waged on, Zhen leapt through a window. It was time for *her* part of the plan.

CHAPTER 19

Inside the vault room, The Chameleon continued her onslaught. Two Komodo dragon guards dragged the latest spirit away as she reached to take a sip of her tea. But before she could relax, a voice boomed from behind a pillar.

"I believe you have something that belongs to me."

It was Po, ready to rumble.

"Can't you even die right?" The Chameleon sneered.

"I'm not going anywhere until you give me that staff back," Po replied.

The Chameleon sighed. She threw the Staff of Wisdom at Po. "Take it. I already have everything I need from it anyway." She took a sip of tea. Then she pursed her lips. "You know, Po, we're not so different."

"Ha. If I only had a dumpling for every time a villain told me how much we had in common," Po replied. "I mean, I'd still probably be hungry, but only because I eat a *lot* of dumplings."

"But this time, it's actually true," The Chameleon said. "All our lives, we were overlooked and underestimated. Yet here we are, each of us at the top of our respective games. That's exactly where I intend to stay."

Po assumed a fighting stance.

"Not if I have anything to do with it," he said. "Let's dance, lizard."

It was on. The Chameleon took many forms in her assault. She transformed into an antelope, slamming Po with her hind legs. Then she was an elephant, knocking Po backward with her trunk. Next, she was a boar, charging at Po, and then she pounced on him, this time as a wolf. She morphed into a bull and bounced Po up and down on her horns. Finally, she assumed the form of Tai Lung.

"*What?*" gasped the real Tai Lung from within his cage.

The Chameleon, in Tai Lung's form, charged at Po. She unleashed a series of Tai Lung's signature moves.

Tai Lung growled. She had taken his moves—without any training!

"Oh, ahhh!" screamed Po.

 119

"Po, I'm stronger than every opponent you've ever faced because I *am* every opponent you've ever faced," The Chameleon said in Tai Lung's voice.

"Is that how I sound?" the real Tai Lung mused out loud. "I don't sound like that . . . do I?"

Po may have been struggling to land a blow against The Chameleon, but he wasn't giving up yet. "You didn't earn those skills. You just stole 'em!" he said.

The real Tai Lung couldn't help but cheer.

"Give him a left . . . a right . . . upper cut!" Tai Lung cried joyfully.

Scott gave him a sidelong glance. "Which one are you rooting for?"

"I'm not sure," Tai Lung replied. He sighed. "This is all very confusing."

The Chameleon—still in the form of Tai Lung—kicked Po into the bars of a cage.

"That's right, Po. And once I send you to the Spirit Realm, I'm going to steal your powers, too!"

"Over my dead body," replied Po.

"Now you're getting it," The Chameleon said.

The battle looked grim for Po. He struggled to make blows against The Chameleon, who was still as nimble and powerful as ever.

Just as she was about to enact her master plan—

WHAM!

Zhen appeared, delivering a flying kick that sent The Chameleon tumbling to the ground.

"Oooh," Po grimaced. That had to hurt!

The Chameleon regained her footing and transformed back into her reptilian self.

"I knew I should have left you to rot in the gutter where you belong," The Chameleon spat at Zhen.

"Better to rot in a gutter than under your thumb," Zhen replied. "Yah!"

Together, Zhen and Po assumed a fighting stance.

"Two against one?" said The Chameleon. "Well now, let's even the odds."

Channeling the powers of some of the spirits, The Chameleon transformed again.

"Master Cobra . . . Master Flying Fox . . . Master Osprey . . . Master Ox . . . Master Wolf." She howled as her form grew, and grew, and grew, until she became a creature made up of all the villains—a Monster Chameleon.

Po couldn't help himself. "That is . . . awesome!" he said. "I mean, it's disturbing, but I mean, it's awesome."

The Monster Chameleon fired her massive tongue at Po and Zhen.

"Look out!" called Zhen.

Po and Zhen dove out of the way just as the Monster Chameleon's tongue shattered parts of the floor. She launched her lethal tongue again but missed, splintering the ceiling above.

"Whoa!" said Po.

In one swift move, the Monster Chameleon snatched up Zhen and bounded for the open roof.

Po was hot on the pursuit. He grabbed the Monster Chameleon's tail and ascended with them.

Now outside, Po sprinted up the Monster Chameleon's back and grabbed hold of her horns. He pulled.

"Noooooo!" howled the Monster Chameleon, plummeting toward the ground. She dove headfirst into a pile of rubble and dropped Zhen.

"Ahhhh!" Zhen screamed as she, too, cascaded down the steep castle cliff.

Po extended his Staff of Wisdom to catch Zhen.

"Gotcha," he said.

Zhen was safe . . . for now.

"Why did you come back?" Po asked Zhen.

Zhen smiled, channeling her inner Po. "It's never too late to do the right thing," she replied.

"You're a real piece of work, you know that?" Po told her.

"Thanks," said Zhen. Then she realized something. "Wait. Is that a compliment or an insult?"

Po shrugged nonchalantly. It was time for *him* to channel his inner Zhen.

"Little of this, little of that."

CHAPTER 20

The pile of rubble where the Monster Chameleon had crashed began to quiver. Slowly, a silhouette rose from the dusty debris.

The Monster Chameleon was back.

"As I said, Po, you and I really are two sides of the same coin," she hissed. "I wonder what would happen if those sides were reversed. If I was the selfless hero and you were the villain."

The Chameleon revealed her new form. It was large, and furry, and powerful . . . this time she had transformed into . . . Po!

"Stand back," Po instructed Zhen. "I'm going to kick my butt." He paused, realizing how that sounded. "Well, not—not my butt, but *her* butt . . . as me. So—so not my—"

"We get it," Zhen cut in.

"Yaaah!" screamed Evil Po from across the room.

Evil Po charged at Po. The two forces collided, causing a gigantic belly wave to emanate out. The force knocked Zhen back into the bars of some nearby cages.

Po ducked, dodged, swung, swatted, chopped, and charged at Evil Po. He was giving the fight all he had.

But still, Po was no match for Evil Po's seemingly infinite arsenal of kung fu skills. Evil Po hurled a flurry of empty cages at Po with ease.

"You can't beat me, Po," said Evil Po. "I can take a thousand forms, but you can only take one—a Dragon Warrior."

With that, Evil Po used Scott the Croc's skill and breathed fire at Po. He quickly dodged the inferno. Across the room, Scott couldn't help but chime in.

"It's cooler when I do it. Right, guys?" No reply from the other prisoners.

Evil Po grabbed another cage and launched it at Po, trapping him inside the magical prison.

"I am the most powerful sorceress that there ever was, is, or will be!"

Po watched as The Chameleon spoke, her words rising from Evil Po's form. And it was in that moment that Po

❖ 125 ❖

realized something—he saw himself in The Chameleon, and not just because of her (dashing) looks.

A winded Zhen sprinted toward Po.

"I can't *bear* her," Po said to Zhen quietly. "But *you* can."

"That's impossible," Zhen replied.

"A wise old turtle once told me that nothing's impossible," said Po.

"The fate of the world hangs in the balance and you're giving me life advice from a turtle?!" Zhen shouted at him.

"You can do this," Po told her. Then he handed her the Staff of Wisdom.

Zhen took the staff reluctantly. But fueled by Po's confidence, her fear slowly turned into determination. She advanced across the room and faced Evil Po.

"And what do you think you're doing?" boomed The Chameleon.

"Finishing what Po started," said Zhen.

The Chameleon offered a slight smile. Her tongue grabbed Zhen and pulled the fox's head backward.

"Oh, please. How many times do I have to tell you? Don't slouch." Nearby, Mr. Ping, Li, and the rest of the thieves and scoundrels materialized onto the scene. They watched as The Chameleon unleashed an onslaught of attacks against Zhen.

"You can't defeat me. I know all your moves," said The Chameleon. After all, Zhen had been trained by her.

But The Chameleon forgot something important— Zhen had also spent time with Po.

"Not this one," Zhen replied confidently.

She performed the same three-strike-upward-smash move that Po had taught her on Fish and Chip's boat.

"Twirl! Strike! Spin. Strike. Fake. Strike! *Skablam!*"

Zhen summoned a chi blast from the staff and propelled it at The Chameleon. It worked! The Chameleon went flying backward.

Po's dads and the thieves cheered as The Chameleon lay there motionless.

"Nice form. You must have had one awesome teacher," said Po, standing beside her.

Zhen's eyes widened with shock. "You could have gotten out of that cage anytime you wanted, you faker!" She shoved Po's shoulder.

"It's not faking. It's *method.*" Po smiled. "Besides, how is a peach pit ever supposed to become a tree if you never give it the chance to grow?"

Zhen hugged Po, and this time, he embraced her back. It was a powerful hug full of love, friendship, and forgiveness.

As they broke apart, The Chameleon rustled. She was dazed and wounded, but not defeated.

"Not to be too judge-y, but it's twirl before spin, fake before thrust, and for the last time, the word is," Po paused, aiming his staff at The Chameleon, "*Skadoosh!*"

The staff slammed down on The Chameleon's tongue. The staff absorbed all of the power The Chameleon had stolen, and returned it to the trapped masters.

"Huh?" The Chameleon was tongue-tied. "No! Noooo!"

The cages opened; the master villain spirits were freed.

"Panda," said Tai Lung as he approached Po. "Maybe Oogway was right about you after all."

Tai Lung bowed in respect, then grabbed The Chameleon by her tongue.

With the staff now back in Po's possession, he drew a yin-yang symbol, representing opposite forces—good and evil, Tai Lung and Po. The symbol left behind a beautiful golden trail that was a portal to the Spirit Realm. The master villains began jumping into the portal.

"See you on the other side, Dragon Warrior," said Tai Lung solemnly.

"Ahhhh!" The Chameleon yelled. She waved her arms, but it was no use—this time, she really *was* defeated. Po and Zhen watched as she and Tai Lung disappeared into the

Spirit Realm.

The ethereal light faded and the portal to the Spirit Realm closed once again.

CHAPTER 21

Morning dawned in the Valley of Peace. Po and Zhen were inside Mr. Ping's noodle restaurant. Now that The Chameleon had been defeated, it was time for Zhen to go back to the Valley of Peace Prison and finish her sentence.

Mr. Ping shoved some food toward Zhen.

"I packed some food for your time in jail. Let's hope it's not your final meal."

Zhen and Po walked off.

"So, I was thinking," Zhen said to Po. "After I serve my time and I'm a free fox again, maybe I'll open one of those acupuncture places that are all the rage."

Po considered this—Zhen's Acupuncture. Acupuncture by Zhen. Charming, but he had other ideas.

130

"I was thinking that you might be better suited for something a little more *hands-on*," he said.

❀ ❀ ❀ ❀ ❀

Master Shifu spat broth in Po's face.

"*The thief?*" Master Shifu said, too stunned to acknowledge the steaming broth dribble down his face.

Po and Zhen stood before him on the training plateau.

"Out of all the candidates you could choose to train as your worthy successor, you chose a *criminal*?"

Po wiped the broth off his face.

"Like I said, you know when you know. Y'know?"

There was a moment of silence.

"Fine," Master Shifu said. "Choose who you want. A thief. A stick. A carrot. I don't even know why I bother. I'm going to go meditate. *Hard*." Then he stormed off.

After Master Shifu disappeared, Po turned to Zhen.

"Don't worry. He'll come around. Probably. Maybe. Doesn't matter."

Zhen looked troubled.

"Are you okay?" asked Po.

"It's just that. . . ." Zhen paused. "Maybe he's right. I'm no hero. What about me says I'm ready for this?"

"Well, as I learned from working in my dad's kitchen, sometimes the greatest dishes come from the most unlikely ingredients."

Zhen took in Po's words of wisdom.

"That's not bad," she said, impressed. "Okay, I see you, Spiritual Leader!"

"Hey, maybe I'm gettin' the hang of this proverb thing," Po said. He paused, deep in thought as he contemplated another. "One shouldn't do a deep squat with a chopstick in one's pocket."

"Maybe you should just stick to kicking butt," Zhen replied quickly.

Meanwhile, out by the Peach Tree of Heavenly Wisdom, Master Shifu was struggling to meditate.

"Inner peace. Inner peace. Inner peace," he quietly intoned to himself.

Nex to him, a brand-new peach tree was sprouting.

Po and Zhen bowed to each other. It was time to start Zhen's training—for real, as the Dragon Warrior.

"Are you ready?" Po asked her.

"Are *you*?"

Po looked at his hand. It *had* been holding the staff. He smiled to himself. Maybe Zhen's thievery would come in handy as the next Dragon Warrior. The Dragon Warrior's foes would never know where their weapons went!

"READY!"

EPILOGUE

So, that's the story—the story of how a masterful panda met a sly fox and they became a team.

In Juniper City, the thieves and scoundrels still lived in the Den of Thieves, with Han as their leader. But as it turns out, they also LOVED to eat noodles and dumplings. They ventured out to the Valley of Peace often and ate at Mr. Ping and Li's restaurant. The restaurant was busier than ever!

Speaking of Juniper City, a few bulls and retired Komodo dragon guards slapped a new poster over Po and Zhen's "wanted" signs. The new poster showed the Dragon Warrior, lavishly holding a bowl of rice. Po's adventures, finally, weren't as regional as he once feared. Granny Boar had a new role, too, in the newly rebuilt tavern—she used her tusks to drum on a large kitchen pot. *Racka tacka racka tacka.* Fish and Chip even took up dancing.

The other Dragon Warrior candidates continued their training. Although they couldn't be the next Dragon Warrior, they could still be awesome.

In the Spirit Realm, Tai Lung and the other masters played jump rope with The Chameleon's tongue.

As for Po and Zhen . . . well, they had a lot of training to do still and many more awesome adventures together.

THE END